REST IN PIECES

As Longarm joined the older and shorter lawman, he saw a spurred and high-heeled boot with fancy stitching lying in a puddle of blood on the hall runner a half-dozen yards from the open door of his hired corner room.

Matilda had described the remains on the rug just inside the door as blown to bits.

Tattered, torn, with its head, both arms, and one leg missing described the horrible sight better. Longarm saw the wardrobe he'd hung his coat in was pockmarked with bloody bone fragments from the floor up to about knee height. There were spatters of blood, crud, and torn-up blue denim stuck to the 'dobe most everywhere that low.

Marshal Higgins nudged the mangled body with a booted toe and said, "Since this can't be you and hotel bellboys don't wear spurs... Then who was this poor cuss?"

DON'T MISS THESE
ALL-ACTION WESTERN SERIES
FROM THE BERKLEY PUBLISHING GROUP

THE GUNSMITH by J. R. Roberts
Clint Adams was a legend among lawmen, outlaws, and ladies.
They called him . . . the Gunsmith.

LONGARM by Tabor Evans
The popular long-running series about U.S. Deputy Marshal
Long—his life, his loves, his fight for justice.

SLOCUM by Jake Logan
Today's longest-running action Western. John Slocum rides a
deadly trail of hot blood and cold steel.

BUSHWHACKERS by B. J. Lanagan
An action-packed series by the creators of Longarm! The rousing
adventures of the most brutal gang of cutthroats ever assembled—
Quantrill's Raiders.

TABOR EVANS

LONGARM
AND THE LADY FROM TOMBSTONE

JOVE BOOKS, NEW YORK

LONGARM AND THE LADY FROM TOMBSTONE

A Jove Book / published by arrangement with
the author

PRINTING HISTORY
Jove edition / July 1999

The Penguin Putnam Inc. World Wide Web site address is
http://www.penguinputnam.com

ISBN: 0-515-12533-4

A JOVE BOOK®
Jove Books are published by The Berkley Publishing Group,
a division of Penguin Putnam Inc.,
375 Hudson Street, New York, New York 10014.
JOVE and the "J" design
are trademarks belonging to Penguin Putnam Inc.

PRINTED IN THE UNITED STATES OF AMERICA

10 9 8 7 6 5 4 3 2 1

Chapter 1

Standing tall, dark, and ugly with his gun slung low, Blacky Barnes had scared many a man skinny. But when he was seated on a fold-down bunk in a patent cell without his gun, it was his turn to feel scared as the federal lawman who'd come to fetch him stared at him through the bars as if he'd been a bug on a pin.

U.S. Deputy Marshal Custis Long of the Denver District Court had done all the paperwork out front before the Arizona turnkey had carried him back to the cells to pick up his federal want. So he already knew they'd arrested the trigger-happy hired gun there in Saguaro Wells after he'd picked a fight in the one whorehouse in town. They'd noticed as he was sleeping off strong drink and a pistol-whipping that his swarthy complexion and black beard matched the wanted fliers on that jasper who'd shot that Indian agent up in the Four Corners Country.

Indian agents being federal employees, and that Southern Ute agency lying just within the borders of Colorado, where it shared corners with Arizona, Utah, and New Mexico, they'd sent Longarm, as he was better known along the Owlhoot Trail, to bring Barnes back to Denver for his trial. So Longarm began by saying, "On your feet and listen tight, you unfortunate cuss."

1

As Blacky Barnes rose to his own considerable height, Longarm told him, "I get an extra day's pay for picking you up, and then I get an extra six cents a mile for your travel expenses added to my own. So as you can see, bringing you back alive ain't likely to make me rich as Mr. John Jacob Astor. So let me count the ways I have to carry you back to Denver."

Blacky Barnes said, "I know your rep, Longarm. How do you figure the odds on my getting off on self-defense?"

Longarm replied not unkindly, "You ain't got a Chinaman's chance. I was talking about us getting there. I got leg irons with my other possibles checked with the stationmaster down to the depot. But I just hate it when folks stare at me and anybody I'm riding with on a train. So let's set us some rules. If you aim to make a break for it betwixt here and Denver, just refuse this offer and we'll say no more about it. If you promise to behave, I may see fit to treat a once-upon-a-time fellow peace officer like a gent and only cuff him to an armrest when I have to leave our seat for any reason. How do you like it so far?"

Before Blacky Barnes could answer, the Arizona lawman who'd taken Longarm back to the cells warned, "He don't deserve no breaks. You'd know that if you'd been with us when it took four of us to bring him in, drunk as a skunk and out of ammunition!"

Longarm smiled thinly and said, "Your boss, the constable up front, already told me how this gent shot the place up and had whores running all over creation. I hardly ever let a prisoner get that drunk as I ride on home with him. Would you mind letting him out so's we could catch that eastbound combination coming through this morning?"

As the turnkey opened up, Blacky Barnes put his black Stetson on and asked, "What about my own possibles? I got a pony, saddle, and saddlebags at the livery up the way."

Longarm said, "I asked about your shit. It's been impounded by Saguaro Wells until future notice. In the unlikely event you ain't hung in Colorado, you can always come back here to claim all but the pony. You couldn't hardly expect to reclaim a pony you stole from the South Ute Agency, could you?''

As they headed out front, Blacky Barnes protested he'd bought a fresh mount fair and square from an Indian trader, only to have a total stranger accuse him as a horse thief, with such harsh words naturally leading to a shooting in self-defense.

Longarm suggested Blacky save it for the judge and jury as, out in the already ferocious morning sunlight, they both heard a train whistle moaning.

After saying his parting thanks to the other town lawmen in the front office, Longarm opened the front door for his prisoner to let them both stride into what felt like a bake oven.

Saguaro Wells, Arizona, was a railroad jerkwater, two days ride north of Tombstone, surrounded by saguaro cactus trees and stirrup-high greasewood for as far as the eye could see, with purple peaks peering over the horizon hither and yon. It was over a hundred in the shade, with only a narrow strip of shade down the east side of a main street running south to the railroad stop. So they hugged the shade as they made their way along the otherwise deserted street. A dusty string of rust-red freight cars blocked the view down Main Street as they headed for the depot. Blacky asked if they meant to board an infernal freight train back to Colorado.

Longarm said, ''I've been studying our timetables. That ain't our eastbound combination. It's the westbound to Yuma on the same tracks. Being the tracks run single-line out betwixt stops, the train you and me will be taking is on a siding just down the line, waiting for a clear track east in half an hour. So that gives us time to check my own baggage out on the platform, and if you're good I'll let you tote some of it for me.''

As they got down to the Saguaro Wells Depot, a glorified

name for little more than an open platform with a combined stationmaster's office and baggage shed at one end, they could see the engine off to their right taking on water from the windmill-pumped tank-tower that gave the tiny town its name. As they reached the sun-silvered open platform, the engine's bell was tolling. Blacky Barnes said, "They're getting set to pull out. Let's watch 'em leave."

Longarm paused in the open glare of the Arizona sun, but said, "Haven't you ever seen a choo choo twain before, little boy? You'll get to see more railroading than this before we're back in Denver, and it's fucking *hot* out here on this platform!"

Then the westbound was starting to move, and Blacky pleaded, "I like to watch trains coming and going. Why don't you just fetch your stuff whilst I stand here like a wooden Indian?"

Longarm replied, "You ain't a wooden Indian. You're my federal prisoner and I'll thank you to act like one. So let's get it on over to yonder baggage master's!"

Longarm half turned to lead the way. That was what Blacky Barnes had been waiting for. It took Longarm the better part of a second to wonder where in thunder Barnes thought he was running to and then get out his .44-40 as he saw the desperate killer was running after that departing freight train.

Longarm yelled, "Halt! I mean it!" and when that didn't work, he aimed low. So Blacky Barnes fell to the splintery wood of the sunbaked platform to start screaming like a woman in labor while he writhed like an earthworm caught by daylight on a brick walk.

Longarm reloaded as he strode down the platform toward Barnes. The departing freight was receding in the distance as half the town seemed to be headed their way. That was the trouble with having to gun a prisoner in a town that had neither a public library nor its own opera house.

The town constable arrived with his own men. That turn-

4

key who'd warned Longarm about Blacky Barnes called out, "I told you so!"

A portly man with a sawbones bag to match his black frock coat and homburg hat grunted himself up on the platform to kneel down by Barnes and say, "Stop your girlish wiggles and let me do something about that bleeding before you leak yourself to death!"

As the older man worked on the wounded prisoner, one of the town lawmen softly confided to Longarm that Doc Plummer was all they had to offer, but that he wasn't a bad sawbones when he was sober.

As if to prove this, Doc Plummer handed Blacky some opium pills and cut open his blood-soaked jeans just below his crotch, on the right side. As he did so he whistled and opined, "A couple of inches higher and you'd be pissing and moaning in soprano. But he missed the femur and main arteries."

One of the lawmen present dryly chided, "Piss-poor shooting, Uncle Sam."

"Am I going to die?" whined the wounded killer.

Doc Plummer shrugged and said, "We're all going to die someday. I ought to have you back on your feet in four to six weeks if your wound don't mortify."

Longarm protested, "Hold on, Doc! Me and him have us a train back to Denver to catch!"

The older man soberly replied, "Then you never should have shot him here in Saguaro Wells. We're talking some serious bed rest over at my clinic whilst he builds his blood pressure back up and we take his temperature every hour on the hour. That's after I irrigate and probe this hole you drilled through his thigh with your dirty bullet you might have had anywhere. Hasn't anybody ever told you more than half of gunshot wounds fester and kill days or even weeks after any shooting?"

Longarm had been in a war one time. So he knew the small-town sawbones was being optimistic when he allowed that the odds were as good as fifty-fifty. Doc

5

Plummer was likely banking on the dry air and sterilizing sunlight. Those bugs Professor Pasteur had taken to warning everyone about were as likely to be lurking inside sweaty jeans on a damp unwashed hide as inside the chambers of a six-gun.

Longarm asked the town constable if someone else would guard Blacky while he wired home for further instructions.

The constable said, "Don't fret yourself, Uncle Sam. We get a heap of trouble riding through on its way to the mushrooming town of Tombstone to the south. Tombstone ain't old enough to have its own rail connections yet. So many a gun waddie gets off at or rides through Saguaro Wells spoiling for trouble, and we often oblige the sons of bitches."

His turnkey explained, "We got it down to rote. If they live, we hold 'em at the jail or chained to a brass bedstead in Doc's combined residence, office, and clinic. Doc's right about it usually taking a leg wound a good month to heal."

The constable said to go right on over to Western Union and send all the wires he wanted. So that was where Longarm went next.

He worded his telegram to his boss tersely, knowing U.S. Marshal Billy Vail was an old fuss about wasting words at a nickel a word.

By the time Longarm was done, the town law and its admiring crowd had carried Blacky Barnes up Main Street to the clinic, wherever it was. So Longarm got his possibles out of the baggage shed in preparation for at least an overnight stay. He knew the same penny-wise and dollar-foolish thrift that inspired all that cussing at Western Union would keep Billy Vail from replying by direct wire when he knew night-letter rates were way cheaper. The hire of a room for the night was likely to be *Longarm's* problem when the time came to settle up for the trip.

At the only hotel in town, catty-corner from the water tower, a cross-ventilated room on a northeast corner could be had for just six bits a night. So Longam carried his McClellan saddle, heavily laden with saddlebags and a '73 Winchester, up to drape across the foot rails of the fair-sized bedstead. Then he shut the jalousied window blinds against the morning sun, pocketed the key, and stepped out in the second-story hall to find himself alone for the moment. So he took out a waterproof match, broke the stem in two, and dropped to one knee to wedge it in the jamb of the closed door, just under the bottom hinge. It was a simple way to be almost certain nobody was waiting for you inside any room you'd thought you'd left locked up securely.

Then he lit a three-for-a-nickel cheroot with what was left of the wax-stemmed Mexican match, and headed downstairs to see if he might manage an early dinner before La Siesta set in.

Anglo and Mexican residents of the Southwest agreed on at least the weather. From high noon to at least three or four in the afternoon, nobody with a lick of sense stepped out into sunlight with high summer coming on.

Keeping his room key in a pocket of a tobacco-tweed frock coat he'd never been expected to wear on government business before the reform Hayes Administration, Longarm asked at the lobby desk about the nearest place to grub.

The skinny old room clerk, relieved that his guest wasn't one of those pests you had to service with his damned key every time he went in or out, suggested the hotel dining room through an archway across the shadowy lobby.

As Longarm passed a grove of potted paper palm trees, he spied a young gal in a dusty riding habit of tan whipcord seated in a club chair. They didn't look directly at one another as he strode on by. It wasn't that sort of hotel.

Longarm sauntered into the almost empty dining room, which was dimly lit by daylight, to take a corner table with his back in a corner. When a dumpy but halfway pretty Mexican waitress came to take his order, Longarm asked in Spanish, or at least in Border Mexican, for fried eggs over chili con carne with a side order of tortillas. He said he'd like black coffee *with* the meal, not *after*. She dimpled down at him and asked where he'd learned to speak such fine Spanish.

He replied in English, "Aw, mush, you don't have to lay it on with a trowel. I tip the same whether you flatter me or not."

She laughed, went to fetch his order, and came back with it in minutes. Longarm had consulted his pocket watch while waiting, and saw the morning heat had made him misjudge the hour some. As hot as it already was, he saw it was only a shade past ten-thirty. That combination he'd heard coming through while he'd been in the Western Union office hadn't left without him as far back as it seemed.

He ate what amounted to a late breakfast or early dinner without hesitation. His belly had been growling, and there was no way to save eggs over chili for later. But he passed on dessert as he sat there smoking a fresh cheroot with his third cup of coffee, saving something to do for later in what was already promising to be one hell of a long morning.

Then that gal in the tan riding habit came in, her tan sombrero hanging down the back of her bolero jacket on its chin cord to leave her upswept light brown hair exposed as she walked right over to him, bold as brass, sat down across from him uninvited, and said right out, "I'd be Lorena Webber from Tombstone. I know who you are and I know what you just did to that gun for hire. Can we talk?"

Longarm decided not to smile. It wasn't easy, as he replied in a politely cautious tone, "I'm listening, ma'am. But no offense, you seem to be talking enough for the both of us so far."

Chapter 2

As Longarm caught the eye of the Mexican waitress, the Anglo gal at his table was saying, "We were riding back from Tucson and planning on shading up here for the afternoon when we heard your gunplay, and I naturally asked around town about it. They tell me you're a U.S. marshal with a rep."

To which Longarm modestly replied, "I'm only a deputy marshal, as my boss, Marshal Billy Vail, is inclined to remind me from time to time. You say *we*, plural, were listening in when I had to discourage that hired gun you mentioned from hopping a freight out of town?"

She smiled across the table and explained, "I rode over to Tucson with some Pima Indians at the suggestion of a part-Pima friend from my school days. You know how shy Pima are around us Saltu. So I left them and their ponies under the ramada at the municipal corral up the street. It was on my old school chum's behalf that we rode all the way in to Tucson. To no avail, it would seem. I've been to see the sheriff of Pima County, and he says Tombstone's too far for him and his boys to mess in domestic disputes. That's what Sheriff Shibell calls the beating and rape of a mere breed, a domestic dispute! And as for the opposite number of your Federal Marshal Vail, I might as well have put a note in a bottle and tossed it in the San Pedro! I couldn't get a single lawman in the territorial capital to listen to me!"

Longarm quietly suggested, "That may because Tucson ain't been the capital since '77, Miss Lorena. But before you ride up to Phoenix, I'm a lawman and I'd be proud to listen, if you'd care to start at the beginning and stay on one track. No offense, but lawmen do tend to duck domestic disputes because they can be so tough to follow!"

The dumpy waitress had drifted over, but seemed to be waiting for a lull in the conversation. So Longarm ordered coffee for the Anglo gal, and Lorena herself allowed she'd take hers *"con azucar pero no crema, por favor."*

As the waitress went to fetch her coffee with sugar, Lorena told Longarm, "I grew up in San Antone. My dad rode with Captain Midnight after the war and did all right. So they sent me to this finishing school back East, where I met Clio Hendersen from these parts. She was a breed. It showed. So she caught more spite from those snobbish Eastern gals than I did, even though her daddy was richer."

"Is this the part-Pima pal we've been talking about?" He asked.

Lorena said, "Yes. Her father was a prospector married to a Mexican-Pima trader's daughter. I mean, really married, in a Papist church by a priest and all."

Longarm nodded and said, "So we're speaking of what the BIA or Bureau of Indian Affairs defines as an Assimilate. A plain citizen who may be part Indian or even all Indian who chooses to live off the government allotment rolls as a self-supporting grown-up. I've more than one such pal, and sometimes they do get snubbed by folks who've nothing to brag on but their complexion. So you two Western gals got to be pals at a snooty Eastern girls' school, and then what?"

She said, "Clio's father was struck by desert lightning over in the Dragoon Mountains. We were in our junior year. So she was never able to graduate. She had to come

10

back out here to salvage the wide-scattered estate her father had left her. He'd owned or held shares in placers and mining properties from Yuma to the headwaters of the Gila. Placers, as you probably know, bottom out after a few productive seasons. A copper sulfide strike that looked promising was tied up in litigation with some long-lost relatives who've dismissed poor Clio as a halfbreed born out of wedlock to a black-sheep squaw man of the family. But he'd filed a silver claim in her name a few months before he was killed. He must have felt in danger over in the Dragoons.''

Longarm dryly replied, ''I don't see why. I know they told old Ed Schieffelin he'd find nothing but his tombstone in such dry Apache-infested country. But we know how *that* turned out. He named his first mine the Tombstone, and followed it up with the Graveyard, the Lucky Cuss, and the Tough Nut, all along the same reef of twenty-two-thousand-dollar-to-the-ton silver ore. But I reckon old Ed and his burro were lucky about those sudden summer storms along all the ridges in these parts.''

Then Longarm frowned thoughtfully and added, ''Hold on, Miss Lorena. Far be it from me to question a lady's age. But if you and your chum Clio were still in college when her daddy found color over in the Dragoons, how come it's Ed Schieffelin who wound up so famous just a few summers back in '77?''

She answered without hesitation, ''Clio's father was killed back in '68. You're right that Ed Schieffelin's more famous Tombstone strike took place in the summer of '77. But it wasn't the first. Ed Schieffelin boasts he found the Tombstone lode by backtracking those dead prospectors he found full of Apache arrows and toting pokes of high-grade ore samples. Such *recent* strikes could only be developed after the army moved Mister Lo, the Poor Indian, up to the San Carlos reserve. Clio's father and some Pima guides were prospecting Apacheria when it was still Apacheria. There were advantages to marrying into a Pima band.''

Longarm nodded soberly and said, "The Pima and their more wandering Papago cousins to the west have less trouble with the Na-déné than most. That's likely because every time a so-called Apache has laid a hand on a Pima or Papago pony, he's drawn back a stump. Neither Pima nor Papago seem anxious to fight anybody, and you can ride right through either if you don't mess with 'em. But ride through a Pima's corn patch or flirt with a Papago's daughter, and you can have a war to the death on your plate."

Lorena said, "Clio told us about her mother's people at school. She said they'd be famous as the Sioux if they weren't so easygoing."

Longarm nodded but said, "Suffice it to say they are, and so they've missed out on a heap of fun with the U.S. Cav. Let's get back to Miss Clio's white father and some Pima pals striking color in '68—where?"

She said, "A place called Chindi Canyon, about twenty miles east of the newer town of Tombstone. You were right about how wild things still were in Apacheria in '68. So while Clio held on to her father's map and filing papers, she didn't get around to trying to claim and prove her Chindi Canyon lode until more recently. She moved from Tucson to Tombstone last winter, meaning to use a town house as her official residence for filing and tax purposes."

"With whose money?" Longarm asked.

Lorena said, "Her own, of course. I told you her father left Clio *other* properties. She was able to sell some of the lower-grade lodes and even placers to larger mining outfits who go in for that sort of thing. I really don't know that much about mining, and her silver lode up in Chindi Canyon is the root of her problems, but not the problem to be resolved. The silver will still be there no matter which side wins, see?"

Longarm replied, "Not hardly. Your old school chum inherited some silver that was tougher to get to until recently. Then what?"

Lorena said, "Clio was the *daughter* of a mining man,

12

not a *mining man.* So she hired a professional mine foreman to ride up into Chindi Canyon with her, assay the surface indications, and tell her just how much she'd be biting off. She said something to me about needing a gold mine to work a silver mine. I'm not sure what that means."

Longarm said, "I am. You have to produce sixteen ounces of silver to make as much as you would on one ounce of gold. After that there are veins of high-grade *gold* ore just sitting out in the dry wide-open stretches of the West. Color is where you find it. But you got to get it to market to *sell* it. A dollar's worth of gold or silver ain't worth hauling back to civilization if it costs you more than a dollar to *do* so. You need water and fuel for your stamping mills within a practical distance from your mine. That's after you buy and haul in all the mining equipment from steam engines to cookstoves for your crew. You have to pay your hardrock men at least three bucks a day whether they're mucking out high-grade or just digging down to it. In sum, it takes a gold mine, not to run but to get a silver mine *started.* So I can see why a mining man's daughter would be smart to hire some experts before she invested another dime, and what did they tell her she had up in Ghost Canyon?"

Lorena said, "High-grade silver sulfide assayed at ten thousand to thirty thousand a ton without drilling deeper. Why did you just call it Ghost Canyon? I told you it was *Chindi* Canyon."

Longarm nodded. "Same deal. Chindi means a ghost, the worse kind of ghost, in Na-déné. They say you meet up with a Chindi around sundown, when the light is tricky and you can't make strangers out too clear. The so-called Apache always fire on anybody they meet around sundown, just in case it's a Chindi. Otherwise, the Chindi is likely to walk right up to you, smiling friendly until it's too late and it's swallowed you whole, if you're lucky. Sometimes Chindi can get downright mean. I can see how a white man and some Pima might have been left to themselves in a canyon named for the very worst breed of Indian spooks. So now your old school chum has a claim worth proving within easy hauling distance of the smelters processing for all those Tombstone mining outfits, and where do *you* fit in, Miss Lorena?''

The brown-haired gal from San Antone said, ''I don't fit into the mining business at all. Clio and I had lost touch after she had to leave school. I graduated, came back to Texas, and married a man I never should have. After my divorce I got some kin who'd still talk to me to grubstake me to a modest herd. Like my daddy, I've done all right with cows. So have a lot of others over on the far side of the Continental Divide. So when I heard there was less competition and a higher market price for beef out *this* way, I headed west, bought more stock, and if only there was more *grass* in this blamed country, I'd be really rich instead of just doing well by now.''

Longarm observed, ''Arizona mining men and all the Indians Uncle Sam has on the rolls out this way ought to add up to high beef prices. Lord knows there never were any buffalo, and the desert deer and bighorns can't take much hunting pressure. So you'd be a budding beef baroness and your old school chum would be on her way to rivaling Ed Schieffelin or at least Leadville Johnnie Brown, but what went wrong?''

The Anglo school chum from Texas said, ''The mining man Clio hired is named Lester Twill. After she thanked him and paid him off for his help, he kissed her and when she slapped his face and told him to get going, he punched her silly and then raped her on the floor.''

Longarm whistled and said, ''You say this Miss Clio hasn't been able to get any help from the law about the brute?''

Lorena shook her head and explained, ''She naturally went to the law right in Tombstone, and Marshal Fred White naturally sent some deputies to haul Lester Twill in. They found him playing cards in the Oriental Saloon. He

14

made no resistance, but produced a marriage certificate naming Clio Twill née Hendersen as his bride, and sheepishly allowed he'd been having trouble with the little woman over the late hours he'd been keeping in town. So guess what those silly Tombstone lawmen told poor Clio!''

Longarm shook his head wearily and replied, ''Don't have to. I'm a lawman. So I know. They told her they had no call to mess in a dumb domestic dispute betwixt a lawfully wedded man and wife unless one or the other seemed in mortal danger.''

He took a thoughtful drag on his cheroot before he added, ''Since the husband she'd filed a complaint about was playing cards well out of her sight, they could hardly say she was in any danger from him.''

Lorena protested, ''But Clio never *married* Lester Twill. She hired him to look over her mining property, and isn't it obvious he's out to jump her claim?''

Longarm managed not to comment on who might have jumping whom, and soberly assured her, ''Looks mighty suspicious to me, ma'am. But to tell the pure truth, if I was packing a badge in Tombstone right now, I'd still tell your old school chum she needed a lawyer, not a lawman. Any lawyer worth his salt would be able to prove or disprove any fool wedding certificate. Like any other civil contract, a wedding certificate needs to be signed by both parties, witnessed by at least two others, and filed with the county clerk. Didn't anyone down Tombstone way tell Miss Clio that much?''

Lorena nodded, with a disgusted expression, and replied, ''They did, and guess what I found over in Tucson when I went to see the county clerk with a sample of Clio Hendersen's handwriting?''

''Don't tell me they have her signature on file?''

''They do. Next to Lester Twill's on an obviously forged wedding certificate! How would you account for that?''

Longarm sighed and said, ''There was this old-time philospher they called William of Occam who advised his stu-

15

dents that when they got stuck with two possible solutions to a puzzle, it was usually safer to go with the least complicated.''

She said impatiently, ''They taught us about Occam's Razor when we studied logic. What simple answer are you suggesting?''

There was no nicer way to put it. So he said, ''The easy answer is that your old school chum and this randy mining man she hired are really married up. It happens, and it's a lady's perogative, or so some say, to change her mind. Have you considered that an old school chum you hadn't seen for years could have fibbed to you a mite?''

Lorena rose, majestic in her wrath, and wailed, ''You men are all alike! Where is a poor woman to turn for justice in world run by such thickheaded brutes?''

Longarm said soothingly, ''To a good lawyer, like I said, Miss Lorena. One or the other has to be lying and if it's him, he's got more gall than a Cheyenne Contrary full of firewater. Where's your old school chum right now, regardless of who's telling the truth?''

She said, ''Hiding from him in yet another canyon with some of her mother's Pima relations, of course. Everyone except you dumb *men* can see what Lester Twill's evil game is. Having forged her name to that fake wedding certificate, and having established he's her misunderstood husband to the law, he means to murder her and claim that rich silver lode in Chindi Canyon for himself as her only living heir!''

Chapter 3

Longarm signaled their waitress as he said, "It's rude to rush a lady, but we need to talk to a lawyer and it's going on siesta time."

Lorena Webber set her half-filled cup aside as she smiled across the table and asked, "We? Does that mean you're going to help us?"

Longarm took their tab from the Mexican gal and commenced to line up the right change on the table as he told the Anglo gal, "It means we ought to see that lawyer before I answer that. I have to allow, though, that I doubt Marshal Vail and I have a dog in any fight down this way."

He left a dime extra, and rose to help her to her feet. As he did so, Lorena asked if it wasn't true that disputed mining claims were a federal matter.

Longarm nodded soberly and replied, "Since Congress passed those uniform rules and regulations and set up the Federal Bureau of Mines back in '72, ma'am. But I wouldn't be honest with you if I said there was a fifty-fifty chance of getting the Bureau of Mines in Phoenix to charge any windmills for you before the fact."

He led her out front, and pointed up the skinny strip of shade with his chin as he explained, "Since '72, claim-jumping has been a federal offense, to be tried in federal courts, once any claim's been *jumped*. I ain't read up on such laws enough to know how you'd convince even one federal prosecutor or a whole grand jury a local marriage ceremony could add up to the jumping of a federal mining claim.''

She insisted, ''But Clio never married Lester Twill, Custis!''

He said, ''Whatever happened was recorded by a local county clerk. I ain't too clear on whether Uncle Sam might have anything to say about such matters in a territory governed at the top by federal appointees. I know incorporated counties in a territory are run just the same as anywhere else. By locally elected county boards, sheriffs, and so on. I read something in some paper about the folks down yonder in Tombstone petitioning to form their own county, distinct from the oversized gerrymander they share with Tucson and, come to study on it, this town of Saguaro Wells. So I'm banking on a local lawyer knowing a lot more than you, me, or even your pal Clio, about the best answer to her awkward fix.''

Then, as they headed up Main Street with her in the shade and him getting beaten on the head by the sun, he added, ''Have you noticed we seem to be being trailed by Indians, ma'am?''

Lorena paused and half turned to regard the two young Pima gals a dozen-odd paces behind them with a sigh. The Pima gals stopped at the same time to just stand there, as if posing for their photographs. A greenhorn might have taken either for Apache in their thigh-length white cotton smocks with shoulder-length hair with bangs. But while a lot of Southwest nations dressed much the same with neither feathers nor fringes, you could tell a Pima from a 'Pache by their moccasins or lack thereof. The two young moon-faced and sloe-eyed gals frozen in place on the plank walk wore rope-soled sandals braided from the desert yucca plants they used for so many purposes. Had they been a couple of 'Pache gals, they'd have had sashes cinched at

18

their waists. But Pima, being true desert dwellers with no mountain hideouts to go home to after a raiding expedition, left their loosely fitting smocks to breathe fresh dry air in and out as they moved or, in this case, just stood there breathing, with their smocks hanging straight down from their chunky tits.

Lorena turned away, and as they started moving again she told him, "Clio told those two to look after me on the trail, and I fear they took her literally. She calls them Topsy and Little Eva."

Longarm was glad he was wearing a broad-brimmed Stetson, but sort of wished for a parasol as he asked, "How come? In *Uncle Tom's Cabin,* wasn't Little Eva the sweet and innocent white kid whilst Topsy was the mischief-making colored one? They look about the same to me, with neither looking all that white or all that colored."

Lorena explained, "I think Clio had their *characters* in mind. Little Eva is inclined to do as she's told. Topsy is inclined to do anything she feels like doing."

"Did you ask either one of them to follow you all over town?" he dryly asked.

She answered simply, "No. As in the book, Little Eva is inclined to follow Topsy and share in the scoldings. Where is this lawyer you were talking about?"

Longarm pointed ahead at the big outline of a six-gun as he said, "Just this side of that gunsmith's sign, Miss Lorena. I get to notice things that others might not. So I spied a lawyer's shingle as I was marching that flighty Blacky Barnes to the railroad, down the other way, and considered how much he'd need a good lawyer as soon as I got him back to Denver."

But when they got there and went on up to the second-story office of A. A. Phillips, Attorney at Law, a gal in her teens with pimples and a pencil in her hair-bun told them they'd just missed her boss. Lawyer Phillips was drawing up a will for a client on the outskirts of town, and the clerk allowed she'd been about to shut down for La Siesta.

Longarm told the kid who he was and where he was staying in town. She said she'd be sure and tell Lawyer Phillips. Then there wasn't anything they could do but head back down the stairs to discover it hadn't gotten any cooler and there was no shade at all on the north-south Main Street now.

Lorena said she'd told her Indian pals she'd come back to shade up with them at the municipal corral. So that was where Longarm walked her, the two Pima gals trailing, as he explained, "Local lawyers often have an in with their county administration. Since you say they told you they had a copy of Clio Hendersen's signature on a marriage form, there's a couple of ways a good lawyer might want to try skinning that cat. Do you have anything with Clio Hendersen's signature on it?"

She said, "No. Why should I? Friends need nothing in writing when they're working together, and both Clio and me agree that crazy Lester Twill must have forged her name to that silly marriage certificate!"

Longarm replied, "Might not be silly if it stands up in probate."

She blinked and asked, "Probate? How could there be any probate hearing while Clio is still . . . Oh, Lord, I see what you mean!"

He said, "Even a good forgery can be contested by the one supposed to have signed it, as long as they're in shape to speak up for themselves. But there ought to be the signatures of at least two witnesses and whoever performed any ceremony."

As they crossed the dusty deserted street toward the sun-silvered rails of a big corral wedged between a livery stable and a smithy, Longarm explained, "No matter who pronounces a couple man and wife, he or she has to do so with powers delegated to them by the local government, unless they're getting married aboard a ship at sea, at a military post, or whatever. So you ought to ask Lawyer Phillips to demand signed and notarized copies of the original forms the fancier certificate was likely transcribed from. Then you'll want him to send a summons to each and every one whose name appears anywhere. If there's nobody by such a name at such-and-such a place, your old school chum is off the hook and her accused rapist is in a bad fix. If even two witnesses are willing to depose under oath that they saw Lester Twill and Miss Clio Hendersen getting hitched, her best bet would be to seek an annulment on whatever grounds Lawyer Phillips can come up with.''

"But she's not *married* to him!" Lorena almost wailed.

Longarm opened a small corral gate meant for humans as he explained, "Don't cut no ice either way if she gets an annulment before he can manage some accident or ague for her. Whether he made the whole deal up or your old school chum's had second thoughts about a hasty move, it's safe to say they ain't *happily* married, and between them they do have a silver mine to fight over.''

As they crossed the empty center corral, with the stock all clustered in the shade of a ramada overhang toward the back, Lorena demanded, "How can you say they have anything *between* them? Can't you see that wicked Lester Twill is out to *inherit* everything once he murders the poor girl?''

Longarm could see the Indians lolling about like Miss Sarah Bernhardt atop the bales of pressed hay rising behind the sheltering stock they were sharing the ramada with. You saw more and bigger ramadas as you rode deeper into siesta country. Ramada translated as a sort of brushwork arbor, and some rustic ramadas were just that. But when you needed an open-sided shady rest for shelter ramadas used the same red tiles that was used on other roofing in the dry and sunny Southwest.

Longarm waited until they were in the shade as well. It felt ten degrees cooler, even with all those flyspecked pony rumps crowding the shade of the overhang. Longarm led the way, elbowing horseflesh out of their way, as he pointed out, "I generally say what I mean, Miss Lorena. By custom of common law, a man gets title to his wife's property as

21

soon as he marries her. It sounds fairer as soon as you realize he'd be responsible for all her debts, public and private, for as long as they both shall live. You say Miss Clio's living with Indians over in the Dragoons?''

She replied, "With members of her mother's clan. Lester Twill would have a time finding her, even with other Pima helping him. Those two girls, Little Eva and Topsy, know the way. I'm not sure all of my Pima escort does. Little Eva and Topsy picked them up for me on this side of Tombstone. Left to their own devices, Pima don't roam as far east as the Dragoons."

They got to the wall of baled and wired hay. An older Pima woman reached a brawny brown arm down to help the white girl up as one of the men bitched about something in the guttural Ho dialect spoken by widely scattered nations the BIA insisted on giving different names to. The Ho themselves thought this was sort of silly. They thought of all human beings as Hada or friends, Saltu or strangers, and Apache, or enemies. First Mexicans and then Anglo Americans had agreed that that Ho term defined the people who called themselves Na-déné pretty well.

When pressed, Ho speakers would allow that Ho Hada were friendly folks like themselves, while red or white strangers could be defined as Ho Saltu or Tai Va Von, who weren't exactly people. The Ho seemed to feel nobody who didn't speak their lingo could be a real friend, but one of the nicest things Longarm had ever been called by some Ho he'd helped was Saltu ka Saltu, or "Stranger Who Is Not a Stranger." He figured that was how this bunch had Lorena Webber down. As she sat up there closer to the roofing, where it had to be cooler, Lorena said her Pima pals were anxious to move on as soon as the sun got lower to the west. They liked to ride at night, and hoped to make it back to their kith and kin this side of Tombstone before it got too hot to ride again. Being desert dwellers, Pima admired the cool and starry desert nights. It gave them an edge over their Na-déné enemies, who'd come down from

22

cloudier climes where nights were more dark and not as safe to be out in. Despite their reps as raiding horse thieves, the Na-déné defined as Navajo were as scared of the dark as little kids, while the so-called Apache had only learned night riding from the Mexicans they'd been messing with before the U.S. War Department ever heard of them. The Pima and their Papago cousins to the southwest were more comfortable at full gallop after ,undown.

Longarm suggested Miss Lorena keep her Pima pals where they were until he could get back to her about Lawyer Phillips, just up the way. When she said she only knew a few words of Ho, and couldn't seem to get anyone to listen to her in any lingo, Longarm warned, "Look, you've ridden high and you've ridden low for your old school chum, and to tell the truth, I'm starting to suspect the reason you ain't been getting anyone to help you. No offense, Miss Lorena, but you have to eat any apple one bite at a time. You can't expect everyone to drop everything else they've been doing and chase after you in shining armor to slay dragons that may or may not *be* there! I've just done more for you and a gal I don't know from Mother Eve because you caught me at a time I had time on my hands. Had I not been stuck here waiting for further orders, I'd have likely been as rude to you as any other busy lawman you'd care to pester with what could be no more than the female ailments of a gal who married in haste and discovered she doesn't really like boys."

"That's a terrible thing to say about any lady!" she blazed.

He growled, "I wasn't finished. I said any lawman worth his salt has to consider false alarms. Having said that, I mean to see that lawyer and ask what you ladies ought to do. As soon as he tells me, I'll get back to you. So don't go riding off before I can. Assuming Lawyer Phillips means to take off for La Siesta with the rest of us, he ought to be back in his office no later than four. It'll take me at least half an hour to lay out your case as I understand it. He'll likely want to talk to you as well. So be here this afternoon when I can get back to you."

She asked, "What if I can't hold these Indian friends?"

He said, "Let 'em ride. Who needs friends that act like a bunch of spoiled brats? Haven't you heard a word I've said, Miss Lorena? You ain't going to get any help from anyone with a lick of sense until you simmer down and commence to act more sensibly. If they ride off on you and you're feeling lonesome, come on over to my hotel and we'll see about hiring another room for you. Neither Lawyer Phillips nor me will be able to do a thing for you if you're riding off by moonlight whilst your old school chum hides out with another bunch of Indians!"

She said she'd try.

He said, "Don't try. *Do* it!" and turned to get under some cover and out of his tweed duds before he melted like a snowman. He shucked his frock coat as he strode back out to Main Street, and draped it over his left arm to leg it back to his hotel in shirtsleeves and vest and to Hell with the new federal dress regulations. He wasn't on duty if it was siesta time, was he?

When he ducked into the lobby of his hotel, it felt ten degrees cooler, but there was nobody behind the desk to ask about telegrams. Longarm suspected the room clerk had retired to cool his own bare ass with business so slow during La Siesta.

Longarm went upstairs and tossed his hat and coat aside before he gingerly opened the window jalousies enough to see he'd been right about the advantages of cross ventilation on the shady side of the second story. He was starting to feel almost human by the time he'd stripped and given himself a sponge bath at the corner washstand. But he was mildly surprised to notice he had an erection as he lay spread-eagle atop the covers, letting the warm but bone-dry desert breeze soak up the moisture from his fresh-scrubbed hide.

He wondered how cool Lorena's hide might feel right

24

now, back at that ramada buzzing with horseflies. He laughed and warned himself to simmer down. He'd just told the pretty little thing one had to eat any apple a bite at a time. So there was no sense panting after her like a mooncalf when it was a well-known fact that women had the deciding vote in such matters.

Chapter 4

South of the Gila and well to the north of it, the heat of the day followed the sun across the sky by less than the usual three hours. So by two in the afternoon, Longarm's corner room was already cooled down to bearable, and he was just bare-ass across the bedstead because nothing downstairs would be open till three or four. Doing nothing when your weren't tired gets tedious. So he was pleasantly distracted when someone rapped on the door.

He rolled his bare feet to the floor and wrapped a hotel towel about his waist as he rose, drew his .44-40 from the rig he'd draped over a bedpost, and went to see who it was.

It was that young gal with skin trouble from the lawyer's office. She turned red in the face all over as she saw more of a man than Queen Victoria might approve of her seeing. But she gamely held out the note from her boss, until Longarm's towel slipped a mite as he was trying to manage the message, side arm, and towel with two hands. He called after her that he was sorry as she went screaming away down the corridor.

A tad red-faced himself, Longarm shut the door after her and let go of the towel entirely so he could put the gun away and read the note.

Lawyer Phillips suggested they meet at his private residence during the last of La Siesta. Longarm suspected no small-town lawyer wanted to lose any business, but that Phillips had to abide by the local custom of shutting down one's regular place of business during La Siesta.

That sounded reasonable to Longarm. So he got dressed, or at least he got dressed to suit Arizona at that time of the year better than the current regulations of the Hayes Reform Administration called for. As he locked up again wearing just his shirt, with no sissy shoestring tie above his cross-draw gun rig, Longarm reflected that no matter what some said about the more hell-for-leather days of old President Grant, nobody had made him wear an infernal *tie* on duty. It seemed a shame they couldn't seem to elect a President who combined free and easy manners with common sense. Longarm wasn't as sure as some that U.S. Grant had been a crook, even though he himself had had to arrest a shit-house full of army and BIA purchasing agents a very good general and hopeless President had appointed.

Finding some shade on the west side of Main Street now, Longarm meant to gather up Lorena Webber along the way to the lawyer's house to the north. But when he got to the municipal corral, he didn't see any sign of the cowgirl and her Indians. A corral hand he scouted up allowed that that bunch of Pima had ridden out less than an hour back, doubtless inspired by the same break in the noonday heat.

Longarm strode on up Main Street, cussing like a sailor who'd found no girls in port after six weeks at sea. For without Lorena Webber, there was no point at all in going to see any lawyer. *He* wasn't the one who needed a possibly expensive lawyer. But Lorena had ridden off, and he had no idea where her pal, Clio Hendersen, had been in the first place!

He had to go on alone. Having pestered Lawyer Phillips and having been treated with consideration by him, Longarm felt he had to explain and allow he was sorry. So he just kept going till he got to a side street suggested in the note, and followed it west till he got to the house with

28

whitewashed 'dobe walls and park-bench-green trim at one end of the second block over.

When he knocked, a moonfaced full-blood dressed like a French maid let him in and tried to manage something in English.

Longarm removed his hat and quietly said, *"Hablo un poquito de español, Señorita."*

So she told him he spoke Spanish well and that her boss had been expecting him if he was El Señor Largo.

Longarm didn't correct her. He knew *largo* meant "Long" in Spanish, and suspected her grasp of English had to be less limited than he'd first suspected. She led him inside, which was furnished more Anglo than the outside, and ushered him into a wallpapered parlor where a handsome older woman with her salt-and-pepper hair pinned up and the bodice of her lavender summer frock filled nicely seemed anxious to serve him some sangria from a pitcher on the rosewood coffee table in front of the settee she was perched on. Longarm figured her for Lawyer Phillips's wife until she introduced herself as Lawyer Phillips.

Longarm managed not to comment on that as he stood there, hat in hand, to explain, "I fear I owe you an apology for wasting your time, ma'am. I ain't the one as needs a lawyer, no offense. I'm a lawman, as I explained to your office gal. I was asked to help two gals from down Tombstone way, and it was me who said they needed a lawyer. So I bear the blame for wasting your time. Neither young gal came right out and *asked* me to get them a lawyer."

Lawyer Phillips patted the dark gray plush beside her and said, "Sit down and have some sangree while you tell me about it. You seem to have impressed my niece Matilda quite a bit."

He managed not to smile at the memory as he sat down beside the older woman, idly wondering what she'd have said or done if it had been *her* in his doorway when the towel slipped a mite.

When she served him a tumbler of what she called san-

29

gree, he forgave what he'd taken for poor Spanish. Sangria was an iced wine punch made with dry sherry and fruit juices. Sangree seemed a gringo version of sangria made with gin and grenadine. But it wasn't bad, once you got over the surprise. Most women seemed to fancy gin more than Maryland rye for some reason.

Knowing he was taking up her time, Longarm offered a terse outline of the case Lorena had presented. Along the way they got to know that his friends called him Custis, while her A. A. stood for Alma Augusta and her friends called her Aggie. By the time he'd finished, they were both smoking as well as sipping her lethal version of a Mexican summer drink.

She waited to see if there was any more for him to say. Then she shook her fine-boned head and said, "You were right about it being no chore for a federal lawman. Speaking as a lawyer, I'm glad the innocent one rode off before I could talk to her. It sounds like a pail of whoppers."

Longarm agreed. "*Somebody* has to be fibbing. What makes you so certain Miss Lorena is so innocent?"

The worldly older woman smiled knowingly and replied, "So you *have* had her! My niece described her as pretty, in a tomboy way. I meant she was probably innocent of *lying*. She admits she wasn't there and so, like you, she only has the word of her old school chum that all this melodramatic nonsense ever took place! I married the wrong man one time. But it seemed much simpler to cut the cards for a friendly annulment."

Longarm said, "I suggested as much. Miss Lorena said this Lester Twill seems too ardent about that silver claim to admit it was all a misunderstanding. How did you talk this other gent into backing off so gracefully, Miss Aggie?"

She shrugged and explained, "It was that or a messy divorce in open court, and few men want it known that they can't get it up enough to do right by their blushing bride. But let's consider that silver deposit. This breed girl, left a lode of silver by her father, would have us believe a mining man she asked for a professional opinion went to all the trouble of somehow filing false reports of a wedding that never took place so that he could—*what?* Murder her and claim her inheritance as his own? Lester Twill was the one who told Clio Hendersen she had a potential silver mine. Wouldn't it have been smarter for him or any other man to say the claim was worthless, wait till any girl gave up on a remote mountain canyon, and simply filed a claim for a silver lode any man could have discovered for *himself*?"

Longarm blew a thoughtful smoke ring and told her, "That sounds mighty raw, and for the record, I ain't never messed with either of the gals we've been talking about."

She shot a narrow stream of smoke through the expanding circle he'd blown before she teasingly replied, "Not as raw as forgery and murder, and I'm glad your motives are so pure. Let's talk about your jurisdiction as a federal lawman."

He sighed and said, "I know. I told Miss Lorena I didn't have any. If either kills the other in the town of Tombstone, the complaint is supposed to be handled by Marshal Fred White. If either one winds up murdered out in the greasewood of an incorporated county, the elected sheriff, old Charlie Shibell, is supposed to investigate. Ain't *nobody* allowed to solve a crime that ain't been committed as yet. If Lester Twill forged those wedding records, it's a matter for the county clerk to take up with the district attorney. If Clio Hendersen is the liar, I can't see anybody arresting her for getting hysterical over a change of heart. Since Lorena Webber's already been over to Tucson to find that the records sort of back old Lester up, the only way to disprove 'em calls for more riding around after witnesses than I'd feel up to if I had the time. I won't *have* the time because I'm waiting on new orders about that federal want I wasn't able to leave with this morning."

Aggie said, "My niece and I only caught the last of that when we came to the windows as the dulcet tones of your six-gun faded away. I heard that hired gun they were holding won't be in shape to travel for some time. Do you think they'll order you to wait here in Saguaro Wells until he recovers?''

Longarm shook his head and confided, ''I ain't got that much leave time coming, and if I did, no offense, I reckon I'd vacation out in Frisco or mayhaps Saint Lou.''

She sighed and said, ''I've noticed how little action there seems to be in Saguaro Wells these days. I've always wanted to visit San Francisco. I could tell you a tale about a beer garden in Saint Lou when I and the world were young and foolish. But to get back to the problem you came to me with, speaking as an Arizona lawyer who knows the ways of the Pima Nation and the Tucson Ring, be glad you have no federal jurisdiction and a fine excuse to let your pretty tomboy work things out.''

He started to ask what she meant. But he didn't have to. He nodded and said, ''I follow your drift. I told her to wait and come along to have this talk with you, Miss Aggie. When somebody floundering in the creek calls for help, you're obliged to hold out a tree limb to them. But if they refuse to grab the other end, like you just said, you've done the right thing and it's up to them to sink or swim.''

He drained the last of his sangree and asked how much he owed her for her time.

She leaned back to let smoke drift out both nostrils as she replied in a dreamy voice, ''We might be able to work something out. My niece described *you* to me as well, quite vividly, and I'd hate to have the skin she does from playing with myself the way she does, the poor thing.''

Longarm soberly replied, ''I noticed she has a skin condition, ma'am. How do you manage such a clear complexion your ownself in a town as quiet as Saguaro Wells?''

She rose to her feet and held out a hand to him as she confided in an earthy tone, ''Very carefully. Would you like me to show you?''

That was not only the best offer he'd had since he'd

arrived in Saguaro Wells. It was likely the *only* offer he was going to get as long as he was stuck in Saguaro Wells. So he rose to the occasion, in more ways than one, and took her dainty hand to follow her into what she described as her sewing room off the parlor. He suspected she had to rest from her sewing a lot when he spied the sheet spread across a velvet chaise longue to protect the upholstry.

Aggie Phillips barred the one door behind them, and commenced to shuck her light summer frock as she said something silly about him never telling anyone over at the saloon about her being a tad overweight. He swore as an enlisted man that her secrets were safe with him. Then they were both undressed and too busy to say anything at all for an-all-too-short slice out of eternity, spent in a Turkish pasha's version of Paradise.

Old Aggie *was* a tad Junoesque in just her black lisle stockings, and her hair was going gray all over. But as he forked himself into the love saddle between her soft welcoming thighs, he was surprised by how tight the gates of Paradise were as she thrust upward with her mature pelvis to inhale him to the roots, moaning, "Oh, Lord, Matilda was right about the way you were hung even when she saw it *soft*!"

He didn't say he owed her niece anything for inspiring such a warm welcome from her more wordly aunt and boss. He was worldly enough to know how bossy some older gals could act when they felt the least bit jealous of a younger gal. But once he'd come in old Aggie the first time, and braced her bare behind on the upsweling curve of the chaise to do it a mighty novel way, he got a little more out of her wild and convenient pose by imagining it was skinny little Matilda taking it that way, combining the advantages of romantic and dog style as he was able to stand upright with his socks planted wide on the rug to ram it all the way in and out with a hand gripping either ankle, while she rolled her head from side to side and fingered her wide-

33

open slit as what sounded like a summer storm rumbled in the distance.

She moaned that she was coming again. He didn't waste breath answering as he idly wondered whether Matilda had pimples all over and whether her smaller tits might bounce in a different rhythm with his thrusts. He decided he liked Matilda's smooth young hide free of any blemishes, and that it didn't matter how tits bounced when a man was fixing to shoot his wad in the only place in the universe that mattered.

Then, just as they were coming, there came a frantic knocking on the fortunately locked door of the small sewing room, and Aggie hissed, "Don't stop! For Christ's sake don't stop!"

So he didn't as the woman he was pleasuring called out in a cool tone that belied the contractions of her innards on Longarm's still-questing shaft, "What is it, Matilda? I can't come to the door right now. You've caught me at an awkward time, half dressed."

The shy little gal with skin troubles called through the door in a more excited tone, "Didn't you hear that explosion down by the depot just now, Aunt Aggie?"

The older woman wrapped her legs around Longarm's bare waist to keep him from pulling out as she grinned up at him dirty and calmly replied, "I think I heard distant thunder a few moments ago. I wasn't paying attention. You say it was an *explosion*, dear?"

Her niece called back, "A dynamite bomb, Aunt Aggie. All the lawmen and half the other men in town are down there talking about it. I thought you'd want to know. Do you recall that Deputy Long you sent me to see a little while ago, Aunt Aggie?"

The woman with her legs around Longarm's naked form languidly called back, "I sure do. You described him so well. What about him, dear?"

Matilda sort of sobbed as she said, "That's who they threw the bomb at. Somebody lobbed a big one into his room during La Siesta and blew him all to bits just now!"

34

Chapter 5

Aggie kept her niece busy in the parlor while Longarm dressed and rolled out a window of the sewing room to drop between close-set 'dobe walls and work his way back to an alley that took him, in turn, a discreet distance before he stepped out on a sunlit street to just mosey on back to his hotel.

He elbowed his way through the crowd gathered out front. That dumpy Mexican waitress from the dining room was in the lobby, talking about him with the room clerk as he strode in. So she screamed and ran off with her apron over her face, while the elderly clerk either fainted or ducked behind his counter.

As Longarm moved up the stairs, the town marshal—they called him Pop Higgins—moved to the second-story landing to see what that Mexican gal had screamed about. When he saw it was Longarm, he gasped, "Judas priest! What have you been doing down yonder whilst we've been looking into your murder up here?"

As Longarm joined the older and shorter lawman, he saw a spurred and high-heeled boot with fancy stitching lying in a puddle of blood on the hall runner a half-dozen yards from the open door of his hired corner room. Other lawmen in the doorway seemed also surprised to see him headed their way with their boss. As Longarm and Pop Higgins got closer, Longarm could see why. Matilda had described the remains on the rug just inside the door as blown to bits. Tattered, torn, with its head, both arms, and one leg missing described the horrible sight better. Beyond the mangled cadaver on the floor, the mattress from the bed had been blown off the springs to lie in a far corner on top of Longarm's McClellan saddle. He saw the wardrobe he'd hung his coat in was pockmarked with bloody bone fragments from the floor up to about knee height. There were spatters of blood, crud, and torn-up blue denim stuck to the 'dobe most everywhere that low. Marshal Higgins nudged the mangled body with a booted toe and said, ''Since this can't be you and hotel bellboys don't wear spurs, how do you like some rider calling on you and waiting here as they lobbed that dynamite bomb in at one or the other of you?''

Longarm dropped to one knee for a closer look at the one spurred riding boot still attached to the singed half-naked body as he said, ''I don't like it at all, Pop. To begin with, I left this room locked up and told them downstairs I was going out. Anybody calling on me politely would have been told I wasn't in here. Somebody sneaking up here with a dynamite bomb would have lit the fuse and wound up to throw it as he kicked the door in.''

''Then who was this poor cuss if he wasn't you or some pal waiting for you to come back?'' asked the town law.

Longarm rose back to his own impressive height as he answered in a matter-of-fact tone, ''The bomber, of course. Who *else* could it be? He might have cut the fuse too short. It's more likely he made the common mistake of using Quick Fuze meant for controlled blasting in hardrock mines. In either case, he kicked harder than he needed to and the door popped open to sort of suck him in, off balance, with a lit bundle of dynamite in his hands.''

A town deputy who'd been listening said, ''Ouch! That must have smarted!''

Pop Higgins nodded slowly, saying, ''That explains the

missing arms and head. Say he staggered in, tripped on that braided rag rug, and fell atop his homemade bomb as it went off. That would explain most of the damage, including the damage to him, taking place down yonder betwixt the bedstead and the doorway.''

Then he added, ''That still don't tell us who he might have been. You boys look about some more for that head, or at least his wallet with some identification true or false. Where are you going now, Longarm?''

The younger but more experienced federal lawman said, ''Up to Doc Plummer's clinic. If Blacky Barnes is still there, he might be willing to shed some light on this other owlhoot rider.''

As he headed down the stairs, Pop Higgins came unstuck to shout, ''Oh, Sweet Jesus, I never thought of that! Jimmy, you and Pablo run along with him and make sure this wasn't meant to draw all of us down this way whilst they took our prisoner away from us!''

So an Anglo deputy in his teens and a stocky Mexican with a sawed-off ten-gauge strode up Main Street with Longarm. It was easier by that time of the afternoon. The buildings to their west cast shade clean out to the middle of the dusty street as it came back to life.

At the clinic, a horse-faced old gal in a brown and white nurse's outfit told them they couldn't pester Blacky Barnes because he wasn't feeling so frisky now that the hydrostatic shock of being shot had worn off and Doc Plummer had said not to feed him any more opium pills until after supper time.

But she gave in with three lawmen growling at the same time, and when they got to Blacky Barnes he seemed rational, no matter how miserable he felt.

He greeted Longarm the way old war vets who'd fought on opposite sides were inclined to, saying, ''I've been thinking mixed thoughts about your brutal ways, Longarm. On the one hand I ought to hate you for gunning me, and every time I feel another pang I do. But even as I lie here, all aching with pain, I have to consider the extra time on this earth you've bought me with that one bitty bullet. When a man gets to counting the numbers of the days he may have left, he gets to really valuing each and every precious one.''

Longarm grabbed a bentwood chair and swung it closer to the head of the brass bedstead to straddle it, facing the prisoner, as he said, ''Somebody just tried to kill me, down the street at my hotel. I hardly know anyone in town, and you'd be the only one I know with any call to have me killed.''

Blacky Barnes stared wistfully up at the pressed-tin ceiling as he replied, ''When a man thinks he's likely to live forever he pays less attention to the sights and sounds all around. Had you not put me in this bed, I'd have never known there were bunches of grapes and maple leaves embossed in every square of that tin ceiling. Can any of you boys tell me why they press them rolls of tin so fancy?''

Longarm said, ''Makes the sheet metal stiffer, without looking as common as the corrugated iron they use on the outside of a roof. I might be able to buy you even more extra days, as a material witness, if you'd care to give us some names to go with your dead sidekick in my hotel room.''

Blacky Barnes said, ''I don't know who you're talking about. I've been fondling my pecker with my free hand, ever so grateful to you for shooting me a tad lower, wishing I'd shot fewer men and kissed more gals in the short time I had any choice in such matters. You can take that last meal they talk about and shove it the night before I mount them thirteen steps. There ain't nothing better they can serve me than a *woman*! A fat old clapped-up whore with a glass eye and a peg leg, if I have my choice between that and the fanciest meal cooked by any French chef. I told that ugly nurse I loved her and wanted to marry up with her, and I meant it. But she's been avoiding me ever since. She knows she's ugly. She just can't see how beautiful every gal and bitty brown sparrow bird on earth can look to a man who may not get to see anything at all, forever and ever in the dark of nowhere!''

Longarm said, "You told us you were headed for Tombstone when they arrested you here in Saguaro Wells. We've heard other gunslicks have been heading for Tombstone with half its paint still wet. Who asked you to come to Tombstone, Blacky?''

The swarthy sweating prisoner handcuffed naked under a single sheet replied, "Nobody. You know why I had to leave Colorado. I heard there was some action in that new mining center and I used to think I was looking for action, when all that really matters in this short life are wine, women, and song, with women first in *this* child's book. I swear, I wouldn't care if that ugly nurse out front told me she had the pox and the blue-balls too. I'd be proud to eat her old ring-dang-do every night for a week before they hang me. It takes nine days for the pox to break out after you've caught it, right?''

Longarm grimaced and said, "I sure wish there was some way I could infest you with leprosy, Blacky. Lord knows you deserve it!''

Then he rose and turned to his fellow lawmen to say, "Dirty talk from this shithead ain't taking me nowheres. I'd be obliged if you boys would make sure nobody takes him out of that bed alive before I can get back.''

Pablo, the Mexican deputy with the scattergun, said, "Nobody with any admiration for ugly women and brown sparrows had better try. But where are you going now, *El Brazo Largo*?''

Longarm said, "When you can't get anything out of a suspect, you question any others you can think of, and Hell hath no fury like a woman scorned. I'll explain when I get back tonight, Lord willing and the creeks don't rise.''

Then he was headed for the livery next to the municipal corral, a tad smug about not picking up on what Pablo had called him.

El Brazo Largo was the translation of "Longarm" bestowed upon him by both the brutal Mexican *rurales* and the Mexican rebels out to overthrow their brutal El Presidente Diaz. If Pablo knew who he was, Longarm knew it was safe to assume every other Mexican in town had heard El Brazo Largo was in town. After that, the question before the house would be which side which Mexican might be on. No tyrant remained in power without *any* admirers, and El Presidente could be generous as well as cruel. So Longarm would have been more comfortable had no Mexicans on either side known about those few dustups he'd had down Mexico way. Longarm hadn't set out to choose sides in the ongoing struggle for a halfway decent Mexican government. But what choice did any decent gringo have when asshole rural police rode into town in their big old gray sombreros to fire on all the men, women, children, and chickens within pistol range?

At the livery Longarm hired a stock saddle to go with the paint pony and spade-bitted bridle they offered at four bits a day. This saved him a trip back to his hotel and more jawing with Pop Higgins. Had he felt the need for a posse and his Winchester, he'd have stopped there for them. But he didn't, so he didn't. He rode out of town to the south by way of another street over, worked his way across the tracks through stirrup-high weeds, and cut across to the wagon trace leading from the railroad town to Tombstone. They'd laid no rails across the desert to the mushrooming Tombstone as yet.

He didn't care. He wasn't headed that far, not without a saddle gun, canteen water, and trail supplies. He'd hired a spunky well-shod barb and Morgan cross and loaded up light with some catching up in mind. He knew most Indians moved slow and steady across cactus country. With any luck they'd make camp before sunset to stuff their faces and rest their mounts during Rattlesnake Time, the hour or so seasoned desert travelers handed over to the sidewinders and desert diamondbacks slithering out of their shady lairs for an evening meal before the ground under their scaly bellies could go from too blamed hot to too cold. All members of the rattlesnake nation hunted best in the tricky light of the gloaming, when they were hard to make out and on the prod for anything warm-blooded that they could sense with those odd pits between their eyes and nostrils. Snakes didn't smell with their nostrils or hear with ears they didn't have. They smelled by tasting the air or dirt in front of them with their forked tongues, and heard other critters' footsteps with their belly scales pressed to the ground. But they saw as well as cats in the dark, and could aim right at a warm moving target such as a pack rat or a man's ankle with those heat-sensing pits some took for extra nostrils. Few Indians who spoke Ho would kill a snake, and just allowing them to rule the desert around sunset saved having to understand them any better.

Not being an Indian who spoke any dialect, and knowing snakes got the hell off an open trail when they felt hoof-beats coming, Longarm hoped to overtake Lorena Webber and her Indians at their sunset trail break. As he rode south, he scouted the dusty wagon ruts ahead for any unshod hoof-prints. That was getting easier as the shadows lengthened with the sun ever lower in the west. It was still too hot, but about as pretty a time for riding as Arizona Territory had to offer.

Southern Arizona shared the Sonora Desert with northern Mexico, and the Sonora was prettier than most deserts because it was mighty old and sort of undecided about how much rain it got. The combination of years and years dry enough for Professor Darwin's notions to work their wonders and the widely spaced but thunderous summer gully-washers had turned some original relation of the common rosebush into dozens and dozens of cactus breeds, from the tiny peyote buttons to the stately saguaro, sprouting its spiny green arms two stories or more. They had cactus plants that looked more like trees, others that sprawled across the ground like spiny crocodiles, and juicy barrel cactus more common in the Sonora than anywhere else in the Southwest. All cactus plants had widespread shallow roots that soaked up all the rain that fell on rare occasions and stored it in what had once been rose stems—only now they acted as both stems and leaves, with what had once been leaves turned to extra thorns.

The stirrup-high stickerbrush, mostly greasewood, creosote bush, and such, looked more like brush in other parts because it had roots that went way the hell down to the permanent water table, thirty to sixty feet deep under most of the Sonora Desert. But a whole lot of water was not to be found, away from widely scattered springs or well sites, between infrequent but ferocious rains. Such rain as they got came mostly with thunder and lightning in high summer. That was why he and Alma Augusta had taken indoor dynamite for distant thunder on such a hot and cloudless day. As Longarm rode along under a cobalt-blue sky, he figured those Indians up ahead would push on faster after dark with a clear sky filled with a new moon and desert stars that seemed close enough to reach up and grab. But where in thunder were the damned Pima in the meantime?

Longarm reined in and moved ahead on foot, leading the paint as he explained, "There ought to be some unshod pony tracks along this fool wagon trace if this is the way they rode for Tombstone."

But he found no such tracks after walking a couple of furlongs with his head held low. So he sighed, got back up in the saddle, and neck-reined, the paint back the way they'd come, explaining, "When there's no Indian sign on a trail, it's a safe bet your Indians took another trail. Miss Lorena said *she* was headed back to Tombstone. But didn't she say those Pima, or most of them, hailed from somewhere *this side* of Tombstone?"

The paint didn't answer. Longarm hadn't expected it to. He heeled it to an uncomfortable but mile-eating trot, and stood in the stirrups high enough to spare his balls as he swore softly and decided, "I might have known a gal who'd tell me a wild illogical story would ride wild and illogical across this damned desert with desert Indian guides! So I still can't say whether that cuss with the dynamite bomb was more interested in her and her pals or Blacky Barnes and *his* pals!''

Chapter 6

They got back to town as the sun was setting. When he returned the paint to the livery, Longarm asked if they had any strange mounts in their stalls or, seeing the same gents managed both, the municipal corral next door. They told him Marshal Higgins had already asked them about that. The mysterious mangled corpse they'd removed from the hotel hadn't left any mount where the law could get at it. He'd either left one with a pal who'd gotten away, or just as likely, come in by rail, meaning to leave the same way. Nobody suspected anyone of walking across the desert in spurred high-heeled riding boots.

Back at the hotel, Longarm found they'd shifted him to a second room down the hall. That dynamite going off in the bomber's grasp hadn't done any structural damage to the thick 'dobe walls and heavy timbers. But the chambermaids allowed it was going to take four or five moppings with lye water to get rid of all that blood soaked into the walls and floorboards.

The new room was cool enough after dark, and he was paid up until the next noon. So he locked his baggage in there for the night, but on advice from his lawyer, he neither stayed there himself nor told another soul where he'd be sleeping while he waited for further instructions from his Denver office.

Old Aggie was even wilder upstairs in her four-poster with less light on the subject. It sure beat all how sensitive gals were, next to men, when it came to the few scars and wrinkles no experienced sex maniac could expect to have avoided. During a breather, as they were sharing a cheroot and conversation, Aggie said she was worried about her niece and assistant, Matilda, damaging herself permanently with some of the objects she used as sex toys. Aggie had caught Matilda at play with ears of corn, bottle gourds, and on one occasion an empty wine bottle. When Longarm dryly asked which end of the bottle Matilda had been screwing herself with, Aggie said, "Don't laugh. The child has a serious problem, and I'm not talking about her pimples. I don't know where she heard or read she could clear up her skin by coming a lot. I told her I'd just had to outgrow skin troubles with no help from the more natural screwing I was getting from some neighbor boys back home. But to tell the truth, I think Matilda just likes to come because it feels good."

Longarm said that was why *he* liked to come as he tickled her fancy with his free hand. Aggie took matters into her own hand as she sighed and said, "You sure have a lot to offer a girl, and I'll bet Matilda has been pretending this was in her instead of, say, a candle or Lord only knows what she's been using since she saw you naked, even though you were soft."

Longarm warned, "It ain't likely to stay soft long enough for us to finish this cheroot if you don't ease off a mite. I hope this talk about your horny niece ain't leading up to a game of Three-in-Boat, Miss Aggie."

She playfully replied, "I might have known you'd suggest something like that, you naughty boy! Have you ever really been in bed with two women at the same time, Custis?"

To which he modestly replied, "Hasn't every man, at

least once? But inviting that love-starved kid to join us wouldn't constitute being in bed with two *women,* and even if it did, to tell the truth, that dream of every growing boy is a mite overrated. It *sounds* like inspired fornication, and you sure can get in some interesting positions. But one of the gals is likely to piss the other one off by suggesting something or refusing to do something just as everyone is feeling really silly. And you tend to find yourself showing off for one gal with the other, instead of just enjoying your fool self, and . . . Why am I going on like this, Miss Aggie? You've surely been in bed with two or more men at the same time by now, right?''

She snapped, ''That's a filthy thing to suggest! What kind of a girl do you think I am?''

He began to stroke her clit faster as he said soothingly, ''The kind I really admire, and you were the one who brought up the subject in the first place.''

She sighed and said, ''Oh, get rid of that silly cheroot and screw me like a show-off!''

So he did, and as he was posting in the saddle of love, Aggie was moaning about always wondering, just wondering, how it might feel if a girl, just once, could have one man coming in her front door while another came in her back door.

He didn't say it would likely feel uncomfortable as well as mighty awkward no matter how well the two gents knew one another. But he never did, because he suspected she might know more about such matters than he did. From the way she came that time, it was possible she was just inspiring herself by talking wild and dirty. He was tempted to suggest they help her niece out with her skin troubles just to see whether Aggie would say yes or faint. He'd cured another gal of a fantasy about beastiality by bringing a damned old wolfhound to her quarters to see if she'd really get down on all fours. Women could be worse than men when it came to making wild wishes. A man who took a wild notion about a knothole or a sheep was inclined to go ahead and *try,* whether it worked or not. It usually didn't. But women were likely to go on dreaming impractical sex dreams because they tended to chicken out before they could discover the notion wasn't practical.

He was starting to have wild wishes by the time he was fixing to come in good old Aggie again. It was easy to picture her as anybody else in the dark, and a nominal virgin in her teens who screwed herself with wine bottles seemed like a maiden in distress his old organ-grinder had a duty to help out. But before he came in even an imaginary waif with skin troubles, Longarm exchanged her for Miss Georgiana Drew, the famous comedienne with a winning smile and bedroom eyes the boys in the back row longed to drown in. For as long as a man was screwing a dream, he might as well dream big! As he shot his wad in the sultry Georgiana Drew, he kissed her good, and as long as she was tonguing him, decided he might as well be kissing Miss Ellen Terry, who played more passionate parts on and off the stage, according to *The Police Gazette.*

Leaving the responsibility of Matilda's hankerings to that wine bottle, Longarm enjoyed a blow job from Miss Lily Langtry, shoved it to Miss Lillian Russel dog-style in the dark, and even got some sleep, before old Aggie was serving him breakfast in bed and asking him how long such a swell situation was likely to last. Lord only knows who *she'd* been screwing in the dark, but from the way she was acting she'd enjoyed all of them.

As he put away her scrambled eggs with bacon, he told her it would depend entirely on the Western Union night letter he was expecting. So she made him do one more with her just in case they'd ordered him on home. The morning sunlight painting tiger stripes on her through the jalousie slats made for a whole new change of lovers.

When he got to the Western Union, walking sort of stiffly, Longarm found he'd guessed right about Billy Vail's reply to his earlier wire about Blacky Barnes. After consulting with Judge Dickerson down the hall in the Denver

Federal Building, old Billy wanted Longarm to come on home for now, and added they could always hang that poor "DELETED BY WESTERN UNION" any time he got well enough to die.

While it was still cool enough for traipsing up and down on Main Street, Longarm arranged for the Saguaro Wells law to move his leg-shot federal want back to the town lockup as soon as he was able to stand up again. He explained they'd be sending *him* or somebody else from Denver in six weeks no matter how Blacky Barnes might feel about it.

Hoping to board the eastbound combination that would be stopping to jerkwater before noon, Longarm returned to his hotel to gather up his baggage. There was nobody behind the desk as he passed through the lobby. He didn't care. He knew they didn't care how guests paid up until noon left, as long as they left *by* noon. He'd found it easiest to just leave the key on the bed with the door unlocked. He'd told them to send any claims for damages to his home office. It wouldn't have been polite to offer the odds on Billy Vail approving a damage claim when the damage had been done by an unknown outlaw. The town of Saguaro Wells would be stuck with the modest hole in Potter's Field if nobody came forward about the shattered son of a bitch. No federal employee had been killed or injured by such an inept display of malicious mischief, and Longarm wasn't about to spend any more time in Cactus Country than he'd have to if he wired home about any possible federal angle.

Reflecting that nobody had jurisdiction to hear the case of a dead man, Longarm went upstairs and along the corridor to the newer room he'd locked his coat and baggage in. He'd naturally wedged another match stem under the bottom hinge. So when he spied it on the floor instead, he thoughtfully drew his .44-40 and gingerly reached for the brass knob with his left hand.

It turned easily and silently. Whoever might have unlocked the door while he was away had left it unlatched.

So Longarm took a deep breath, twisted the knob, and slid his back the other way along the wall as he flung the door open wide.

Neither of the two young gals reclining across his hired bedstead like recently fed tabby cats moved a muscle as they just stared up at him like well-fed tabby cats. Lots of Indian gals had eyes like that.

His mysterious guests were Little Eva and Topsy, those two Pima gals Lorena Webber had pointed out the day before. Their loose thin cotton smocks came down to just above their knees when they were on their feet. Longarm idly wondered whether either noticed how much tawny thigh both were showing as they lay sideways on the bedding. He was pretty sure the one whose bare-plucked pussy was showing had to be the one Clio Hendersen had named Topsy.

Holstering his side arm as he moved to close the door, Longarm got tired of waiting for them to say something, and so, even knowing it was considered rude to get right to the point with most Indians, he asked with a smile, ''To what might I owe the honor of this visit, ladies?''

The one whose private parts were concealed by the hem of her high-riding smock said, ''We are very cross with you. We have been waiting, waiting, and where have you been since we rode back here?''

It would have been rude to tell a *white* gal it was none of her business. So he asked how long they'd been waiting for him.

Little Eva, he assumed, said, ''We rode in just after midnight. One of the maids who works here is Ho Hada. She told us you had gone out. She said she did not know when you would be back. We asked her to let us wait for you here in your room.''

Longarm nodded and said, ''I see she did. Before I take you both downstairs and get them to serve you some food and drink, would you mind telling me what this is all about? Did Miss Lorena Webber send you back with some message for me? Is she here in town herself?''

The sassier one called Topsy got up, allowing her smock to cover her more modestly, as she said, ''Let's go. We are hungry and thirsty. The Saltu girl our kinswoman, Porevo, told us to guide to Tucson is dead. We thought we ought to tell you before we ride home to say this to Porevo.''

Longarm blinked in confusion as it came to him that they had to mean Clio Hendersen when they used her Pima name, Porevo, while the term Saltu had to refer to the white gal, Lorena Webber, they'd been assigned to by their breed boss lady. As Little Eva rolled off the bedstead as well, Longarm said, ''Hold on! You say Miss Lorena is dead? When did she die? How did it happen?''

Topsy came over to take his hand like a trusting, or hungry, child, saying, ''Let's go eat. Somebody shot Porevo's Saltu friend just after dark last night. They were waiting for us out on the range with a buffalo rifle. So they must have known which way we'd be riding, and they didn't want that Saltu girl to come back from here. We thought at first they were after *all* of us. So we lay flat in the greaswood for a long time.''

Little Eva explained, ''After some of the men with us circled wide to kill the killers, we knew they were not there. Honaduka, the eldest of the Ho Hada who were helping us, said they would carry the dead girl on to the Saltu Taibo in Tombstone. He said he thought we ought to come back here and tell you what happened. Why did you offer us food and drink if you did not want to?''

He apologized, and led the two of them downstairs and into the hotel dining room, his mind in a whirl and mad as hell.

There were no other patrons at the tables at that awkward hour. So he led the Pima gals to a corner table and sat them down as he asked more questions and got fuzzy answers about what must have been a few minutes of total confusion lit by no more than starlight and muzzle flashes. Topsy said they'd been shot at more than once, but that only Lorena

Webber had been hit, smack over the left brow.

Little Eva demurely volunteered, "It blew her hat and half her skull away. She could not have felt it. She still pissed a lot as she lay on the ground with her skirts up around her waist. Why do Saltu women wear cotton pants under such long skirts? What are they trying to hide from everybody?"

That Mexican waitress had likely peeped out from the kitchen and told on them. A burly Anglo in a cook's apron came out, frowning, to tell Longarm, "We don't serve Indians here, mister."

Longarm got back to his feet, smiling wolfishly, as he replied in as firm a tone, "That's all right. None of us wants to eat an Indian. We'll have three mugs of coffee, and seeing I've eaten, two bowls of chili con carne with a dozen tortillas on the side."

The man who worked there said, "I don't think you understand me, mister. Them squaws can't eat here. They ain't welcome. How can I put it any plainer than that?"

Longarm reached out to grab a big fistful of shirtfront and twist while he lifted the beefy cuss on his toes, growling, "You're the one who can't seem to understand, friend. I want that coffee and grub on the double, or I'm going to wreck this joint and mop up the mess with your face. Can *I* put it any plainer than *that*?"

The other white man allowed that Pima were more refined than the Indians the management must have had in mind, and said he'd get cracking with their orders as soon as Longarm let go of him.

As he vanished into the kitchen, the mollified Longarm rejoined his Pima guests at the table and told them to pay no mind to the way some greenhorns talked.

Topsy grinned like her naughty namesake in that book and said she wished the silly Saltu had held firm so they could have watched Saltu Ka Saltu wreck the joint.

Longarm cautiously asked who'd told them he was that particular Saltu. Little Eva demurely replied, "The elders speak of you fondly and often. You were the one who took sides with our nation when bad Tai Van Von or Saltu Taibo told lies to Little Big Eyes about those allotments they never delivered to us after they had been paid to do this. We knew who you had to be as soon as that dead girl told us a great metal star who could be trusted was here in Saguaro Wells.''

''What are we going to do about them shooting that Saltu girl who wanted to help our Porevo?'' Topsy asked.

It was a good question. As that Mexican waitress came from the kitchen with a loaded tray and a worried expression, Longarm told the dusky gals he was with, ''First we coffee and grub you ladies. Then we go over to the Western Union and I send another wire to my boss back in Denver.''

As the waitress spread their orders on the checkered cloth, Topsy grabbed a tortilla to stuff in her mouth as Little Eva asked how long it would take to get an answer from his chief.

Longarm growled, ''Ain't waiting for no answer. Some rascals for some reasons unknown tried to kill a federal lawman right after he'd been asked for help. Then they did kill the woman who'd come to said federal agent for help. So I'd say that makes the case federal, whether she needed federal help or not!''

Chapter 7

When he asked at the Western Union, they told Longarm
they'd handled many a telegram since he'd come to town
a morning earlier. A lot of wires had been sent or picked
up by travelers passing on through by rail, coach, or on
their own. He didn't put himself to the trouble of arguing
them into letting him go over the telegraph blanks that
would have been sent or received in code by anyone he'd
be really interested in.

As he walked up Main Street to the municipal corral with
the two Pima gals, the one called Little Eva tugged at a
braided yucca cord around her neck to haul a buckskin poke
up from between her cupcake tits. He was surprised and
mildly chagrined when she took out a gold double eagle
and dropped the rest of her poke out of sight again. He
didn't say anything. In his day he'd paid for many a white
woman's meal in the mistaken belief she was broke, and
he'd been wondering how they were managing their ponies.

When they got to the corral, he found out they hadn't
been riding ponies. They'd left six Cordovan saddle mules
there to await their return from his hotel. Little Eva explained that two of the spare mules were meant for him.
He didn't argue. He knew that while most cowboys and
many Indians scorned the horse-sized Spanish jackass, with

55

the so-called Apache inclined to *eat* it, folks like the Pima who knew the desert better knew why the Spaniards had brought the blend of Arab horse and North African burro to the dried parts of the New World in the first place.

Spanish saddle mules could take more heat and carry a heavier load farther on less fodder and water than a horse, and while a mule might not step as fancy, it stepped sure-footed, across rougher range than the wild pony ranged on, when left to its druthers.

Longarm had naturally toted his saddle and saddlebags along with his stuffy tweed coat lashed atop the bedroll behind the cantle and his Winchester '73 sort of flopping around. So as Little Eva settled up with a corral hand, Longarm saddled one of the mules with his own gear to get it out of the way and help the gals with their own.

Indians rode bareback if they had to, but favored saddles they'd made, begged, borrowed, or stolen for the same reasons everyone else who rode did. Despite all the romantic claptrap about Mister Lo, the poor Indian, being a natural cavalryman, the average U.S. Cavalry trooper didn't fall off his mount as often as a bareback-riding Indian in a mounted skirmish. Indian-fighting cavalry heroes owed much of their reps to the oats they fed their bigger and faster mounts and those stirrups that kept them aboard the same while they were swinging with their sabers at Indians on tired scrub ponies.

Being as pragmatic as most Ho speakers, the Pima gals had somewhere come by a couple of Mexican roping saddles with exposed cottonwood trees or frames, outfited with four canteens apiece and those big square buckskin envelopes white mountain men called parfleches, even though that was wrong.

The literal translation of parfleche from the French-Canadian was "rawhide," and most Indians dressed and decorated their leather hold-alls to be water resisting. Trail grub and changes of duds wouldn't travel too well in real raw, unprocessed critter-skin. Most all of the Indian nations made some version of the parfleche because you only had to see one, one time, to see how they worked and how handy they were.

He didn't ask either Pima gal what you called a parfleche in *their* dialect. He didn't care. Ho was tough enough when you tried to remember more important words such as *"Ai"* for "Yes" or *"Ka"* for "No." The widespread Uto-Aztec language, as the professors called it, wasn't half as tough to learn as Na-déné, or Apache-Navaho, but it was still one son of a bitch for a white man to get his tongue around, and what the hell, both gals spoke fair English.

So he got the three of them saddled up and they rode out, with each rider leading a spare mount and the roguish Topsy leading Longarm and Little Eva in turn. He was glad when they'd made the short distance across the tracks and out of town. For there'd been early morning foot traffic to either side and Topsy was riding astride, with the hem of her cotton shift high enough to expose her bare brown rump, had not the wooden cantle of her Mexican saddle risen barely enough to preserve some shred of modesty. Longarm tried not to picture the way the open slit running the length of the saddle's seat had to be sort of smiling toothlessly up at her own gaping slot, seeing the way her bare thighs were parted. Well-brought-up Victorian gals in skirts rode sidesaddle with just such considerations in mind.

Longarm warned himself not to dwell on anyone's crotch, looking forward to the forty miles or more to Tombstone and no telling how long a ride over to that canyon in the Dragoons where Clio Hendersen might or might not still be waiting. He'd found Indian gals neither more nor less willing as white gals on average, with both breeds as well supplied with blushing wallflowers and total sluts. But white men were inclined to get themselves in trouble around Indians because they misread some pragmatic facts of Indian life.

Queen Victoria and her admirers didn't live anything like the most advanced Indians, left to their own ways and old-time religions. So it didn't mean near as much when an Indian gal let you see her bare-ass or taking a pee where there wasn't any modern plumbing. Pueblos and such managed to have private bedrooms on occasion. But most Indians lived so jammed together, it was just more practical to look the other way when someone on the next sleeping mat was changing duds or even having sex. It was understood without having to be said that another man who rolled around the fire for some slap-and-tickle with the same gal, just because she'd given him a hard-on, was as likely to have his head handed to him as a white man going next door to trifle with his neighbor's wife or daughter. Indians tended to savvy notions such as adultery, incest, or rape and take them just as seriously as anyone else. They just didn't try to pretend that nobody in their band ever took a shit or got laid.

As he rode out across the desert after the bare-assed Topsy, he saw why he hadn't been able to cut their trail the evening before. The wagon trace from the railroad town to Tombstone had been laid out with wagon wheels in mind. He saw they were following what had to be an old game trail, and he could only marvel at the Pima Nation's uncharted but memorized road map of the vast expanses they roamed.

Unlike the true diggers of the Great Basin to the north, the Pima and their Papago cousins did a little farming, a little hunting, a little gathering of wild desert bounty, and so on. There wasn't enough of anything in Cactus Country to get by on alone. So when they weren't cultivating tiny patches of beans, corn, and squash, or gathering the seasonal fruits of different desert plants, mostly the sickly-sweet red fruits of the stately saguaro, they were hunting anything from the desert bighorn down to chuckwalla or, as they called the chicken-flavored reptiles, *chacahuala*. The bigger game with hooves didn't care to break through fresh caliche or desert pavement between browse. The distinctive light gray crust left by the evaporation of hard water between rains crunched loud to give a critter's furtive night travel away, and the sharp edges of broken-through caliche could get rough on a hairy hide after a few furlongs. So bighorn, deer, javelina, and such tended to follow one another's footsteps where the crud had already been broken through to the softer desert dirt below, and mules traveled easier along such game trails as well.

During a trail break he asked the Pima gals where they'd been hit by sniper fire. Little Eva said that thanks to their late start, they'd had to shelter from the noonday sun well this side of the site of that ambush they'd ridden into after dark. Longarm glanced up to see a few scattered clouds overhead with some serious thunderheads rising off to the south. But he was commencing to feel the heat, even riding in shirtsleeves, with his Stetson shading his face. You didn't feel sweaty on the Sonora Desert. The hot dry air sucked sweat right out of your pores, and likely cooled you some, even though it was tough to take comfort in such abstract desert lore since it just kept on getting hotter.

Topsy, out in front, cut across protesting caliche crust toward a grove of cholla on the north slope of a gentle rise. Longarm was an Anglo rider, but he didn't ask why. Anglo, Mexican, and many Indian riders stayed the hell away from cholla, or jumping cactus, with good reason. The brittle cactus pads were fuzzed with barbed spines meant to catch and cling to anything brushing by, and while it wasn't true cholla pads really *sprang* on man or beast to dig in with fish hooks or porcupine quills, they surely *seemed* to.

But the desert-dwelling nations knew cholla pads would leave you be if you never really touched them. And the cholla was a "tree cactus," with growth habits a lot like its very distant cousins, the tree rose and crab apple. So a grove of cholla offered much the same shade as a grove of crab apples, even if such "fruit" as it offered was mean as hell if you brushed lightly against a single hairy spine.

Longarm had shaded up under cholla before. He drew his Winchester from its saddle boot as he dismounted, and used the steel muzzle to bat cholla pads away as he opened a seven-foot-high entrance through the ferocious wall of hellish fuzz. Once he had, the shady interior of the fair-sized cactus grove was as safe to enter as any apple orchard under its overhead canopy. All six mules, being desert-bred, knew enough to lower their heads and flatten their jackass ears as Longarm and the Pima gals led them in out of the noonday sun.

Once near the middle, where it was safer to stand, the three of them tethered and unsaddled the mules they'd last ridden, placing all three saddles upside down in the grit to dry before they watered and nose-bagged all the stock. Longarm noticed this took most of the canteens the three of them had been packing. He didn't say anything. It was their desert.

He washed down a can of beans from his own saddle with a can of tomato preserves. He offered both gals a taste, but they said they'd tried *dukapah* before and liked their home-baked *pikipenat* with plain water better. When Little Eva offered him a taste of what sure looked like rolled-up cardboard, it turned out to taste like sweet hominy grits. He'd thought *penat* meant something like sweetness or honey in Ho. *Dukapah,* for his own, translated something like "shit-for-food."

The three of them had spread saddle blankets in the shade to laze on during their enforced siesta. The same evaporation that brought a lot of lime and some silica to the surface cemented the birdcage grit left by the dry winds to the same thin brittle desert pavement you crunched most everywhere else. But by this time, they'd turned a good-sized patch in the middle of the grove back to more comfortable birdcage gravel they could stretch out on. The two Pima gals accepted his after-dinner smokes, but waited until they'd both shucked their cotton shifts off over their heads before they lit up to recline on their blankets, facing him, like saloon paintings of naked Egyptian ladies. He didn't say anything about this. Neither gal looked the least bit flirty as they calmly puffed on their cheroots, and maybe Pima carried such casual notions of proper attire a tad further than some Indians he knew better. Thanks to that last early morning demand from good old Aggie back in Saguaro Wells, he was able to control his own feelings some. But it was likely just as well for those delightfully built little things that he wasn't a really horny white man, or even an Indian from another nation.

He recalled a brawl breaking out in a Cheyenne camp he'd spent a night with up on the North Range. The dog soldiers had been beating this young crooked lancer for mounting a gal in her sleep, until the older women had protested that a gal who sleeps outdoors, totally bare-ass, just because it's a hot night, is asking to be mounted by *some* damned body. Most nations held that a naked gal was supposed to at least look shy and turn her old ring-dang-do the other way in public.

Longarm tried not to stare at either of their hairless pubic mounds as he reflected that they'd all be stuck there for at least three or four hours, Lord willing and it cooled off some by late afternoon. He knew the gals wanted to bed down until sunset and ride on in the cool of evening. But he wanted to scout that ambush site, and he had to repeat himself when Topsy allowed that Pima menfolk who knew the desert better had already lost the trail of the rider who'd killed Lenora Webber.

She said they'd naturally cut the trail of a shod pony coming and going across virgin pavement to lie in wait for them. But the killer had ridden mostly to or fro along the wagon trace from Saguaro Wells to Tombstone, and one shod pony left prints a lot like any other. Topsy said one of the Pima men had found and picked up the brass from the killer's buffalo rifle. But when Longarm asked her the brand name and powder charge, she only recalled that Honaduka had said it had been a buffalo rifle and Honaduka was old and wise.

Longarm took off his hat and then his shirt to spread

beside his guns at the head of the blanket as it got ever hotter, even in the shade. He nursed the little water they had left by making small talk with the oddly named Pima gals. When pressed, they confessed to more Indian-sounding names. But Topsy said what sounded to his white ear like ''Tahkooteen'' could come out really dirty if you pronounced it that way. Little Eva's even tougher Pima name was something like ''Ta-Soon-Da-Hippy,'' and when she said it meant an innocent young thing who didn't know any better, Longarm allowed that Little Eva worked as well.

It was easier to see they weren't twins, or even likely as close as two sisters, once they were out of those identical white cotton outfits. Little Eva was built fuller and softer than the somewhat taller and more wiry Topsy. They'd both put their coin purses aside with their shifts and rope-soled sandals. So there was nothing to distract a man from ad-miring their equally shapely but pleasantly different naked breasts. Longarm tried gazing up through the cactus pads at the tiny triangles of desert sky above.

He noticed they were more gray than blue, and said so. Topsy put a hand idly to her crotch as if to make sure it was still there as she replied in a lazy purr, ''We may have an afternoon thunderstorm. I hope we have an afternoon thunderstorm. It's too hot for fucking right now, but I just love to fuck on a wet blanket after a nice cool soak under the rain-feathered wings of the *waigon*! Don't you?''

To which Longarm could only cautiously reply, knowing he'd be on the trail with them a spell, ''I reckon, if *waigon* is your handle for that old thunderbird. But what about this other lady? Ain't she likely to be as wet and chilled when that storm blows over?''

Little Eva demurely replied, ''I don't mind if you fuck her first. It makes me feel more like it when I watch others fucking for a time, and you *are* man enough for *both* of us, aren't you, Saltu ka Saltu?''

Chapter 8

The gents who sold merchandise knew women did most of
the household shopping and paid the most for their duds.
For while it didn't hurt a pretty gal to have some class,
most men paid way more attention to what she looked like.
It didn't hurt a famous man to be good-looking either, but
women were more inclined to admire a man because they'd
heard a lot about him, or a new dress because it was from
Paris, France. So Longarm had run into other ladies who'd
read about him in the *Rocky Mountain News*, or heard him
referred to as El Brazo Largo along the border, Wasichu
Wastey in Lakota circles, or as in this case, Saltu ka Saltu.
So the Lord only knows how many gals he'd never met
were bragging about his old organ-grinder inside them. He
knew for a fact that old James Butler Hickok had been
faithful to bourbon, poker, and his wife, Miss Agnes Lake,
the circus gal. But thanks to all those stories about him as
Wild Bill in the penny-dreadful press, all sorts of aging
belles now claimed to have been his one true love, with the
crazy Calamity Jane declaring him the sire of that daughter
she'd had out of wedlock in '73 up in Montana Territory,
even though Hickok had been appearing in Buffalo Bill's
road show, *Scouts of the Plains,* after having served as the
law in Abilene, Kansas, during any possible time when the

homely drab could have managed to get knocked up.

Longarm had slept with a Mexican gal who'd sworn she was the one true love of Billy the Kid, even though young Henry McCarty, Billy Antrim, or whatever, had been unknown anywhere while she'd been at that Mexican convent school. And naturally, he'd once had the handsome grass widow of the one and original Deadwood Dick, who'd never existed off the pages of a magazine published in London Town.

He hoped both those gals praised his lovemaking half as much as the others had bragged about Billy and Dick. He figured they likely would. It made for a better brag if the famous cuss who'd sworn you were his own and only had long-donged you half to death.

Sprawled under the cholla canopy with two naked gals who'd heard such gossip about him, Longarm consoled himself with the thought that his performance wouldn't really matter, even if old Aggie had left him in poor shape to perform. Little Eva and especially Topsy were likely to bestow a full twelve inches on him around future campfires whether he could get it up or not, and so this thought, naturally, inspired a certain tingle in his loins as, somewhere in the distance, they heard a roll of thunder.

Longarm got up to move over by his airing saddle, turn it right side up, then unlash the bedroll. He unrolled it, and took the ground cloth upslope to where the cholla pads grew lower, before he knelt on the desert pavement to scoop a shallow depression and line it with the water-proofed canvas. The naked Pima gals had trailed after him to watch, talking to one another in their guttural native language. Little Eva switched to English to say, "We think you are doing that so rainwater will pool there for our empty canteens. That is a new trick we have never seen. You are wiser than Shehekey. You call him Old Man Coyote."

To which Longarm modestly replied, "Your folks don't have Mr. Goodyear's rubberfied canvas. Since I do, I figured any rain ought to run off the hung-down cholla here. How soon do you reckon it might start to rain?''

Little Eva answered simply, "Now," as the three of them blinked at the chalk-white glare all around and heard the ear-spitting crash of thunder that followed close on the lightning's heels.

It was raining like hell as Longarm ran back to his saddle to lay his guns across the seat, place his hat atop them, and proceed to get out of his boots and duds while they were still halfway dry.

In his hurry he forgot the naked Indian ladies. But they were both watching with interest as he tossed the cover tarp of his bedroll on the pile, already goose fleshed by the rain running down through the cactus canopy in pissy streams. Both gals laughed and clapped their hands as he turned to see how his improvised water-catcher up the slop was doing. When he saw how they were staring down at his still-undecided shaft, he grinned and said, "You ain't seen nothing yet. But let me make sure I piled enough grit under the downslope end. One can always get laid, but dying of thirst can be a bother."

As he knelt on his naked knees to observe the fair-sized catchment basin, the rubberized canvas was already good and wet. He'd left a low spot at the downslope end so the first dusty water could run off the canvas. He moved over to it and shoved more grit under that with his bare hands. Topsy laughed and said, "The water you are catching now is clean and cold. Let's fuck."

He said, "First things first. We're getting more rain than I was expecting."

They followed him back to his tarp-draped saddle, and watched with interest as Longarm scooped a shallow ditch all around the pile and then ran a drainage channel down the gentle slope as, sure enough, the water that would have run under the edges of his tarp proceeded to fill his shallow but vital moat. The Pima gals scampered over to do the same for their spread-out saddle blankets. Both blankets as well as their Mexican saddles were already soaking wet. But as Topsy observed while scooping, it could be a bother to have rainwater running under one's bare bouncing behind.

The three of them had moved just in time, Longarm saw by the lightning flashes, now almost constant, punctuated by almost total darkness under the rain and wind-lashed canopy. For water was running down the long gentle slope in sheets, unable to soak in much where the caliche still cemented the fine gravel grains together. A heap of the Sonora Desert's troubles were caused as much by the lay of the land and its chemistry as the loco climate.

Such widely spaced but horrendous summer storms as they were now having scared even the desert-dwelling Indians because that thunderbird up yonder was dead serious and aimed its lightning to kill. Summer lightning was the next-most deadly danger to man or beast on the Sonora. The unexpected peril that killed the *most* out on any desert was unexpected *water*. More folks had died by *drowning* in the dry Southwest than from any other cause, including Indians and rattlesnakes combined.

Thanks to knowing better than to camp in a wash or more treacherous playa, Longarm and the Pima gals didn't have to worry about a flash flood or what had seemed a vast open expanse suddenly turning into a big old lake with the shores too far away to swim for. But while the lightning *usually* struck higher targets on higher ground, there just weren't any sure bets once the old thunderbird got to flapping above you. So Longarm wasn't surprised when there came a sizzle-snap way too close for comfort and one of the gals grabbed hold of him in the dark wet tingle that followed to throw them both off balance.

Longarm fought to stay on his feet as he hung on to the slippery wet naked flesh of the whimpering gal. Then he wondered why anyone would want to struggle like that at a time like that, and just let the two of them fall to the wet dirt, and if they missed a blanket, who the hell cared?

She didn't seem to mind the way the rain-soaked bird-cage grit felt under her bare behind as Longarm rolled his wet hips between her wet welcoming thighs. But as he entered her contrastingly warm slippery innards, a voice from the dark wetness all around wailed, "That's not fair! You were supposed to fuck *me* first!"

Longarm kissed the one he'd mounted some more and said, "Howdy, Little Eva. I know you said you wanted to watch for a spell before you decided, but . . ."

"I've decided! I've decided!" the shorter and softer one sobbed as she dug her bare heels into the caliche to thrust up passionately in time with his friendly thrusts. Then Topsy was hunkered down with a bare heel dug in to either side of his bobbing butt as she straddled it to pound his wet back with her fists, wailing, "Hurry! Hurry and then do *me,* or I'll have to start without you!"

But the one called Little Eva was made to be savored by any mortal man with the good fortune to feel so intimate with her in a pouring rain. So Longarm held her tight and kissed her French as he slid up and down her soft slippery charms, happy as a he-frog mating in an irrigation ditch. From the way she slithered about under him all the while, she seemed to be enjoying the novelty as well. Longarm had long since learned never to ask a good lay how she'd gotten so good. Now and again they'd tell you the truth, and sometimes the truth could sound disgusting.

They came as another lightning bolt threatened to sizzle them together as one big smoking gob. Then she allowed that her butt would feel better if she could brush it off and get some wet wool under them.

Longarm agreed that sounded swell, and rolled off to help her to her feet. He located a saddle blanket during a flash, and led the way. He flopped to the soggy blanket and rolled on his back, still hard. So he naturally thought that was Little Eva moving to straddle his hips with her heels and squat down to impale herself some more on his rain-washed erection.

But one of the things that kept Longarm single was the simple fact that no two women were exactly the same anywhere, Lord love 'em, so he knew without waiting for the next lightning flash that it was Topsy taking her own turn with him, and he was glad he'd had Little Eva to begin with. For while the shorter and softer Little Eva was built as tight as any man had the right to expect, the more muscular Topsy was even tighter!

Stronger too, he could tell as she moved up and down in that dancing position, inhaling and exhaling his raging erection in a way to make many a whore offering French lessons envious. So he just lay back and enjoyed it as rainwater cascaded off her nipples to cool his brow, until Little Eva cuddled down beside him to Kiss his lips and haul his free hand across the wet wool to pet her bare bald pussy.

It wasn't true Indians had no face or body hair. They had about as much as Chinese, and could grow mustaches if they put their minds to it, as any visitor to Old Mexico could attest. They simply tended to pluck such sparse body hair as they had, the way some white ladies of fashion tended to pluck their eyebrows. But as Topsy slid her literally naked crotch up and down his merry-go-round pole, Longarm reflected on how little plucked eyebrows did for a lover, next to a baby-smooth wet snatch. This made him idly wonder what it might feel like if neither the man nor the woman had any hair down yonder, and though he knew he wasn't about to start shaving down yonder, the mental picture inspired some upward thrusts that Topsy seemed grateful for.

Then it was Little Eva's turn again, and so it went until the rain let up as suddenly as had began, although they still heard thunder in the distance as the late afternoon sun came back out to start sucking the Sonora dry again before nightfall.

But meanwhile, the cactus roots all around and all their canteens had been replenished, and neither the Pima gals nor their saddle mules seemed to mind the cool damp cotton shifts or wool saddle blankets as they got ready to ride on.

By sundown they were all bone dry and starting to feel sunbaked again. Then the sun went down, and they broke trail and put away their light suppers while the snakes were at their most dangerous. By the time they rode on, it was uncomfortably cold under the desert stars. So Longarm put on his frock coat, and the gals broke out wraps woven from strips of rabbit fur with just such evenings in mind.

When they came to the stretch where Lorena Webber had been shot from ambush, Little Eva pointed out, and Longarm agreed, that between the darkness and all that sudden rain, there'd be little point in his scouting for signs their own keen-eyed Honaduka might have missed.

They rode on, and on, breaking now and again, with a spell of three-on-a-blanket atop a rise, toward morning when the gals said they were cold and the coming dawn could bring more heat than desire.

Then sunrise caught them out on an open playa that had likely been a shallow lake the afternoon before, and by the time they'd crossed it he for one was riding so hot in his shirtsleeves that he'd have had to say no if his Pima pals had been the free-loving Victoria Woodhull and her naughty kid sister, Miss Tennessee. For though the Woodhull gals had done *something* to inspire Commodore Vanderbilt's generous support of Victoria's run for President, as old and fat as the late commodore had been, Longarm was sure not even a blow job from such experts could inspire *him* that morning.

He might have been right. He didn't make love to either of the Pima gals until they broke trail under a north-facing rock shelter on the western slopes of the San Pedro Valley they were now following. They all got a few winks of sleep. They doubtless needed more. When Longarm asked how far they were from those other Pima who'd tagged along to escort them and the murdered white gal, Lorena Webber, Little Eva told him, "They are closer, on this side of the

San Pedro. But why do you want us to take you there? They know nothing, nothing about who killed the Saltu friend of Porevo. We thought you would want to ride on into Tombstone and see if your own friends have caught anybody yet."

Longarm allowed that made sense, up to a point. Then he told her, "I wanted to talk to this Porevo, or Clio Hendersen as we'll call her, to ask more about her trouble with that Lester Twill who claims to be her husband and joint owner of her silver mine. Miss Lorena said she was hiding out with your own band on the other side of Tombstone."

Little Eva said, "She is. We can't take you to our secret canyon on our slope of the Dragoons. It would not be a secret if Saltu knew where it was."

Topsy said, "We were told to leave you and the Saltu girl to wait in Tombstone at her house, if she had lived. We shall have to leave you somewhere else in Tombstone while we ride on to tell Porevo all that has happened. If she wants to see you she will have to ride into Tombstone herself. Porevo is one of us, almost, but the old ones are not going to let her give away any secrets of our nation."

Longarm nodded and said, "I follow your drift. So how far might we be from Tombstone Town right now?"

Topsy said, "Not far. Maybe a four-hour ride as your people count your heartbeats for some reason. But the sun is still high and none of us can say if we'll ever meet again. So why don't we get really hot and dirty together before we have to ride on?"

To which Longarm could only reply that he couldn't think of anything hotter or dirtier than what they'd been doing. So they had a lot of fun showing him, and if the truth be told, so did he.

Chapter 9

What with one thing and another, they forded the shallow San Pedro near sundown and rode into Tombstone after dark. Longarm would wonder about that later on. He'd long since learned that his own sex wasn't alone in planning ahead while having wild and crazy times on a saddle blanket.

The spanking-new mushroom town of Tombstone stayed up all night to cater to the round-the-clock shifts working the four main silver mines paying for all the fuss. They were still talking about incorporating or carving a new county out of the vast sprawl still run by the Tucson Ring. So the proposed city hall of Tombstone was still a vacant lot on Fremont Street, close to where the rival daily papers, the *Epitaph* and *Nugget*, glared across at one another.

But despite its smell of fresh paint and the cactus still standing in some vacant lots, the main streets of Tombstone were lamplit all night, and lamplight gleamed from many a window of the five hundred or more buildings erected so far.

Half a dozen of these buildings were hotels. There were more like a dozen boardinghouses, if all of them were really boardinghouses. Nobody knew for certain how many whorehouses there might be in any town frequented by cattle and mining men who seldom compared notes.

There were sixteen licensed saloons, balanced by four churches of the Congregational, Episcopal, Methodist, and Roman Catholic notions. There were four theaters for those less inclined to praying, and one bank for those smart enough to save their money.

There were naturally eight corral and livery outfits, and a few score outlets for grub gun, dynamite, and dentistry serving close to ten thousand souls of all sizes, shapes, and colors.

Except where mine adits, stamping mills, and such broke up the pattern, Tombsone was laid out as a gridiron of oversized blocks to occupy at least a quarter-section sloping gently to the west. Those streets running north and south were numbered from First to Seventh, reading from the west. The east-west cross streets had been given names, with Safford, Fremont, Allan, and Toughnut the ones to remember. Fourth and Fremont met as the center of the business district.

Leaving the Pima gals with the mules at the Dexter Corral and Livery, Longarm took himself and his baggage to the Cosmopolitan Hotel. The room he hired wasn't old enough to have gotten really dirty or buggy. He put on his frock coat against the night chill and locked up, to rejoin his Pima pals and tell them where they could reach him if they wanted to.

They must not have wanted to. When he got back to the Dexter Corral, the hired help told him the Pima gals had paid up and ridden on with all six of those mules.

So Longarm ambled back to Hafford's Saloon near his hotel to wash down some ham on rye with a scuttle of needled beer as he reflected on the perfidity of the unfair sex with a wistful smile.

He knew that despite all their vapors and faints, women were more practical than any man could hope to be while screwing. That was how women made the best spies and whores. Sometimes both. That old Belle Siddons who'd spied for the Confederacy by cajoling secrets out of Union officers had wound up running "Madam Vestal's" house of ill repute in Denver after the war. So Longarm figured the warm-natured Pima gals had planned all along to leave him stranded on foot in the town of Tombstone while they rode on to tell Clio Hendersen where he might be found.

That sounded fair, when you studied on it. If the Pima elders had forbidden Clio to entertain visitors at a secret Pima hideout, she'd do better meeting them in town. And any paper records, true or false, would be easier to scout for this far west of the Dragoons.

It was too late to pester anyone about the mortal remains of poor little Lorena Webber, and he wasn't sure Billy Vail would want him to make the usual courtesy call on the local law.

To begin with, he'd ridden down here more or less on his own. His Denver District Court would have no jurisdiction, even if he could prove a local resident had shot another local resident with a buffalo rifle. The crime had occurred on federal open range, it was true, but Billy Vail's opposite number in Tucson was the U.S. marshal with the better claim on such a crime. Longarm had passed through the new town with its confused power structure before. So while, as far as he knew, old Fred White would still be the law, within the limits of Tombstone Township, they were still bitterly divided on who they'd want for county sheriff come the fall elections. So it might be best to let sleeping dogs lie until he had a better handle on what in blue blazes was really going on. Once he had somebody lined up to arrest, he could cut the proper local lawmen in on it. If he never caught up with anybody worth arresting by the time he had to go back to transport his federal want back to Denver, there'd be no need to see this printed in either the *Epitaph* or *Nugget.* Murder cases went that way sometimes, and Billy Vail sure got vexed when a deputy looked dumb in the *Denver Post,* which tended to reprint anything exciting that happened anywhere west of the Mississippi.

Some mining men and a cowhand were playing poker at a nearby table with a walking corpse in the black suit, frill-front shirt, and brocaded silk vest he'd already chosen for his funeral. They had met in the past. So Longarm rose to move with his scuttle of beer before they could lock eyes. Doc Holliday was a tedious bullshit artist when he was sober, and downright mean when he was liquored up. New boomtowns such as Tombstone tended to draw such pests the way fresh shit draws flies, and the newspaper men who kept track of such pests had already commenced to count the ways a man could get his fool self shot in Tombstone. The *Epitaph* ran a column, reprinted in other papers, called "Death's Doings in Tombstone." Young Johnny Clum, who'd just started to publish the *Epitaph*, had behaved more sensibly as an Indian agent. It sure beat all how a man who'd stood up for the occasional mischief of the San Carlos Apache could get so fired up about a drunken cowboy in the same frame of mind. The newer *Epitaph*'s editorial policy favored the mining and business interests and their need for law and order, while the year-older *Nugget* sided with its first subscribers, the cattlemen of the San Pedro Valley, to take a boys-will-be-boys view of shot-out lamplights. But on those rare occasions when the *Nugget* called a mean drunk a menace to society, the *Epitaph* was likely to praise him as a pillar of the community. So the varying accounts of such locally notorious gents as Buckskin Frank, Curly Bill, Doc Holliday, the Earp brothers, or Johnny Ringo were being recorded in a manner to really confuse the historians of the future.

Longarm didn't want to be featured in either paper. So he found a new seat on the far side of the crowd, facing away from the consumptive Holliday. The last time Longarm had passed through, Doc's unpredictable pal, Morgan Earp, was riding shotgun for the Tucson Stage, a comfortable distance off. Longarm tried to avoid unpredictable gents with budding reps for gunplay because no matter what one said or did around them, some fool reporter was likely to write more bullshit about the both of you. Like the late James Butler Hickok, Longarm had been named in newspaper accounts of excitement that had simply never happened. They never paid a newspaper stringer for reporting that nothing at all had happened when a rider with a rep had passed through on his way to yet some other destination. So Longarm shuddered to think what either Tombstone paper would make of his more serious visit to their fair city.

Longarm felt about ready to pack it in for the night with a few swigs of suds still left in his scuttle. But as he pushed what was left of his beer away and reached in his shirt pocket for a smoke, a rat-faced individual in a derby hat and wilted linen suit that had started out white sat down across from him, uninvited, to declare he was Edward Trevor Esquire, Attorney at Law, but his friends called him Ted.

Longarm stared thoughtfully at the distasteful little man for a spell before he replied, "Assuming you must know who I am, I ain't sure whether I'm pleased to meet you or not, Counselor. Who might you be working for and how did you know I was in town?"

Trevor said, "You're as cool as they say. I wired an associate in Saguaro Wells as soon as I heard about the death of Lorena Webber this morning. I knew she'd ridden off to recruit outside help for her pal, that crazy breed gal Clio Hendersen."

Longarm said, "Then I take it you're siding with her sworn enemy, or husband, depending on who you ask. Before you say anything silly, I ain't made up my mind who's fibbing. I'm more worried about a young gal getting murdered on federal open range just after some sorry son of a bitch tried to kill a federal agent she'd turned to for help."

Lawyer Trevor soothingly replied, "That attempt to blow you up with dynamite was in the *Epitaph* this morning. Editor Clum seems to admire you for some reason, Longarm. As soon as I heard you were heading our way, I started to keep an eye out for you, and there are only so many places in a town this size to keep an eye on. I haven't looked you up to say anything silly. My own client, Mr. Lester Twill from Tucson, now residing here in Tombstone, has some federal offenses of his own to report. To begin with, he was never paid for surveying, assaying, and refiling a lapsed silver sulfide strike with our Uncle Sam's Bureau of Mines, Interior Department, as in Washington, D.C.''

Longarm growled, "I know mining claims on all public or private lands are federal. I was told Twill proved out that claim to the east in Chindi Canyon on contract, then stated he was married up with the lady who'd hired him and wasn't going to charge anybody for the silver lode he owned, jointly, with the gal he claimed as his wife. So make up your minds, Counselor. You can't send yourself a bill."

Trevor grinned, exposing yellowed teeth more suited to a beaver than a rat, as he smugly replied, "I was hoping you'd see it that way too. Clio Hendersen claims she never married Lester Twill and that, in fact, he raped her on what he thought was their wedding night. If we conceed that outrageous possibility, just for the sake of argument, where's the evidence she ever paid him for his time and trouble as a mere mining expert for hire?"

Longarm shrugged and said, "I ain't got it. Like I told the late Lorena Webber, it seems to me the two of them ought to take their mutually impossible tales before a civil court, with each side laying out all its cards. He says he married her and has the papers to back his claim. She says he's trying to jump her claim with a forged flimflam. One or the other has to be lying. But it seems to me any civil court should take less than seventy-two hours to have one or the other in deep shit for perjury at the least, and forgery if the shoe fits the other foot."

Lawyer Trevor said, "I agree. I've been trying to serve a summons on Clio Twill née Hendersen for days. Her husband, Lester Twill, is here in town and ready to appear in court with bells on. He swears the marriage certificate he's provided for my brief will stand up in any court of law. But his wife keeps ducking us, owing him money for his goods and services *on a federal claim* if she never really married him. So with you as a witness . . ."

"Back off!" Longarm cut in, flatly stating, "I told you I ain't took sides as yet. Do yourself and your client a real favor and don't piss me off with silly bullshit. If the withholding of wages on open range was a federal offense, we'd be too busy collecting back pay for trail herders to go after stock thieves. You have to keep a sense of proportion when enforcing any laws. The infernal congressmen who keep passing new federal laws never seem to worry about anyone enforcing them. I just told you I was keeping an open mind about the domestic dispute betwixt that unhappy couple. If I come across anything that proves one side or the other to be in the right, I'll be proud to say so, under oath if need be.

"But the federal case I'm down this way to investigate may or may not have some thing to do with that silver lode in Chindi Canyon. Somebody tried to kill me right after I'd talked to Lorena Webber. Then somebody killed Lorena Webber right after she'd talked to me. That's all I know for certain. But I'm treating it as a federal case until somebody shows me I shouldn't."

Lawyer Trevor shrugged and said, "That's no skin off my client's nose. He'd never spoken to Lorena Webber to the day she'd died. He'd naturally heard she was going around accusing him of abusing another gal she'd gone to school with. But he knew that was his poor crazy wife's doing. He didn't blame a gal he'd never met for buying such wild tales about him. And besides, he'd have even less call to go after you or any other lawman they'd been pestering about him."

Longarm agreed that made sense if Lester Twill was the one telling the truth. Lawyer Trevor agreed he'd hold the cuss while Longarm put the cuffs on if *Clio Hendersen* was telling the truth. Then, since they had no way of proving anything that night in Hafford's Saloon, they parted more or less friendly.

The dumb conversation had dried Longarm's whistle enough for him to drain the last of his suds and set the scuttle aside. But as he rose, yet another slithery night crawler, this one dressed more cow, came over to him, eyes darting from side to side, to ask if Longarm was Custis Long and whether he knew Johnny Ringo or not.

Longarm cautiously replied, "I've heard tell of him. Might have howdied him in the Oriental when I was bellied up to the bar with Curly Bill, as a matter of fact. What about him?"

The furtive young cowhand almost whispered, "They say his name's really Rhinegold, but that it ain't too safe to let on you know this."

Longarm said, "I try to discuss religion as seldom as possible, and there's no law against a man calling his fool self Jingle Bells if he's a mind to. So what about the sensitive soul who'd like to be remembered as Johnny Ringo?"

The uneasy messenger gulped and said, "I hope you understand I'm only doing as Johnny Ringo asked. I ain't at feud with nobody!"

Longarm patiently insisted, "Give me the damned message and you have my word I won't slap your wrist. What might Johnny Ringo want of me, damn it?"

The hand the notorious Ringo had sent said, "I don't know. But he wants you to meet him at the Crystal Palace and he wants you to come alone."

Chapter 10

Like many another Crystal Palace in the American West, the one in Tombstone didn't look anything like the glorified greenhouse built in London Town for that grand exhibition. But the Tombstone Crystal Palace was about as big as saloons needed to be if they had stage entertainment as well as gambling on the main floor and whoring in the cribs upstairs. Longarm had been there on an earlier visit to the brawling mushroom town, and so he thought it an odd sort of setting for an ambush.

On the other hand, they said Johnny Ringo had once gunned a man in another saloon for refusing to drink with him, and hardly anybody set up an ambush where the target was likely to suspect one.

Knowing this, Longarm left Hafford's Saloon by way of an alley exit, and worked on over to the Crystal Palace the long and darker way round, sneaking into yet another side door and up the back stairs to where he could gaze down at the crowd assembled along the bar from on high, like one of the soiled doves who nested up yonder.

Thanks to that earlier time in the Oriental, Longarm was able to single Johnny Ringo out from the others along the bar, and the jasper seemed to be alone as he kept a casual eye on the front door.

Johnny Ringo was a saturnine individual in his late thirties who, unlike some so-called "two gun" men, really wore his two Schofield .45-28's both at once in two separate cartridge belts criss-crossed between his belly button and bladder. He favored almost black but trail-dusted riding duds. Like most of the cattlemen you saw in the new town of Tombstone, Ringo bunked on a cow spread out from town and rode in when the spirit moved him. There was nothing responsible for a cowhand to *do* in Tombstone.

Wondering what Johnny Ringo might be up to in town that night, Longarm worked his way down the stairs. A bouncer stationed at the foot of the stairs gave him an odd look and asked, "When did you go up and which one were you screwing?"

Longarm quietly allowed he was a health inspector, checking for crab lice, and pushed on without looking back when the bouncer made a rude remark about his mother.

Some gals were doing an Irish jig and singing about an old sod they'd likely never seen on the lamplit stage as Longarm worked his way across the floor between the tables with his double derringer palmed in one big fist. But when Johnny Ringo saw him coming, and seemed to recognize him as well, the notorious gunslinger smiled boyishly and called out, "Howdy. Thanks for coming. I didn't want to meet you in Hafford's because that pesky John Clum and other Black Republicans hang out there. I wanted this to be a more private meeting, see?"

Longarm bellied up to the bar beside him and replied, "I do now. Were you trying to scare the shit out of me, or does that just come with being . . . whatever the hell you are."

Johnny Ringo laughed lightly and replied, "Think of me as the black sheep of a tediously scholarly family. If I told you the college I was thrown out of, you'd have a better idea of my true nature. Suffice it to say, I can tell a man to fuck himself in Latin, Greek, or Hebrew, and on occasion I feel compelled to do so. Has it ever occurred to you, when you've had enough to drink, that there's no fucking *point* to the cruel joke existence has played on us all?''

Longarm said, ''I reckon, but what's the answer if you ain't enough of a man to play the cards you've been dealt and see the game out? I read all that poetry Mister Khay-yám wrote about moving fingers and how you may as well molest children and steal from poor boxes, because for all you know tomorrow may never come, when I was just a kid. But then I noticed that nine times out of ten tomorrow *does* come, and wouldn't you feel silly if the sunrise caught you with your hand in the cookie jar?''

Ringo sighed and said, ''I have and you're right, it feels silly. What are you having?''

Longarm said, ''Maryland rye with a beer chaser, if you're paying. How come you're paying, Mr. Ringo, and how come you talk country one minute and like a college professor the next?''

The mysterious Ringo said, ''Call me Johnny. The Texas accent can save a lot of bother when you ride with Texans and have as short a temper as I've been blessed with.''

He signaled the barkeep, who came over pronto, and told him to make sure Longarm's rye was Maryland rye if he valued the glass on his back-bar. Then Ringo turned back to Longarm and explained, ''I don't know what you've heard about me. I'm sure a lot I've heard about you is bullshit too. I work for Mr. N. H. Clanton at Lewis Springs up near Galeyville. According to that fucking *Epitaph*, that makes me a member of the so-called Clanton Gang.''

The barkeep slid the large and smaller glasses across the bar to Longarm, who quietly replied, ''I've been to Gal-eyville. So I don't blame you boys for riding on in to Tombstone. It ain't that much farther, and it has to be more worth the riding after a hard day's work. What sort of work might you *do* for Old Man Clanton, Johnny?''

Ringo sighed and said, ''You *have* been reading the *Ep-itaph*. Poor old N. H. gets a better break from the *Nugget*. The cattlemen were here first and it wasn't easy. What do you know about raising cows here in Cactus Country, Pilgrim?''

Longarm belted the rye and chased it with some beer before he said, "That was good stuff. You just said it wasn't easy. The beef cow is not a beast of the desert, and if it was, you gents are too far from the usual markets to make it worth your whiles—if it wasn't for one of the main industries of Arizona Territory, Mister Lo, that Poor Old Indian.''

Johnny Ringo laughed and said, "You *have* been reading up on the subject. N. H. Clanton and the other cattle folk in these parts sell most of their beef to the Bureau of Indian Affairs to feed the Indians, or to the War Department to feed the soldiers they have out here to keep the Indians eating their suppers like good children. Since all these silver camps have broken out around here, there's a growing local trade in fresh beef to go with the mining men's potatoes. But N. H. Clanton has a government contract to supply beef on the hoof to the Apache up to the San Carlos Agency, and getting enough beef to those ungrateful Indians can be a bother in this climate.''

Longarm sipped more suds before he quietly asked, "Did John Clum make up his mind your boss was a crook whilst he was still the agent up at San Carlos or after he moved down here to Tombstone?''

Ringo shrugged and casually replied, "Everyone in the beef industry has to cut a few corners now and then. It's not true that N. H. steals stock from other Arizona outfits. You have my word as a former gentleman that the few heads of beef we've obtained informally came from south of the border. N. H. is a Texan who lost kin at the Alamo, you see.''

Longarm smiled thinly and said, "I'm commencing to. This summer, with Victorio raiding along the border and both the Mexican *federales* and U.S. Cav out after him, would be a piss-poor time for the Clantons to go searching for strays down Mexico way.''

Then he finished his beer chaser and asked, "Is there any point to this conversation, friend?"

Johnny Ringo said, "There is. We heard Miss Lorena Webber had come to you for help just before somebody gunned her, out on the Sonora."

Longarm nodded soberly and replied, "She did. What might that have to do with Old Man Clanton and the rest of you informal cattlemen?"

Ringo said, "Miss Lorena hailed from Texas. The Clantons had to leave Texas when she was a tyke. But old N. H. remembered her family with fond respect as gentlefolk of quality. So when she first came out here with her own little herd, he ordered us all to keep an eye on Miss Lorena and her livestock."

That Irish jig ended in a round of applause and catcalls, giving Longarm time to consider his reply while a more exciting lady in blue velvet came out to bust loose with an aria from *Carmen,* in French, even though Miss Carmen was supposed to be a Spanish Gypsy. Longarm let her trill some before he turned back to Johnny Ringo to say, "Let me see if I can guess. Old Man Clanton's worried about what's to become of Miss Lorena's herd, now that Miss Lorena has been shot in the head by a person or persons unknown?"

Ringo softly replied, "Something like that. He'd naturally offer her estate a fair price, if only we knew who that might *be*. We were hoping *you* might know, seeing you were with her at the end."

Longarm shook his head and said, "Close, but no cigar. Her business with me up in Saguaro Wells had nothing to do with beef futures, and we never talked about any kith or kin she had out this way, save for a gal in the mining business, not the cattle business. I'd told her I couldn't see how I'd be any use to either of them, and she left me up yonder to come back here. As you likely heard, she was ambushed along the way. I was nowheres near. But now that I'm here, you can tell Old Man Clanton we do share the same interest in the estate of the late Lorena Webber. You can tell him I'm going to take it personal as all hell if one unbranded dogie turns up missing betwixt now and a proper probate hearing on all the goods and chattels the murdered gal might have left, and I do mean every last corset stay and dust rag in or about any property she held title to in town or country.''

"Do you know who'd stand to inherit off the poor little gal?" asked the two-gun rider for a reputed cattle thief.

Longarm shook his head and confessed, "Nope. Never considered it my own beeswax until just now. But since Old Man Clanton's asked a man who knows Latin, Greek, and Hebrew to speak for him, you can tell him for me in plain English that I'll likely be looking into his government beef contracts as well as where he and all his riders might have been the night before last when somebody tried to kill me and managed to kill Lorena Webber!"

Johnny Ringo soberly replied, "I'll tell N. H. But he ain't going to like it. Hasn't it occurred to you that if anyone riding for old N. H. Clanton had been told to do you in, we wouldn't be having this dumb conversation? When *we* set out to finish somebody off, we generally do the job right!"

Longarm stared through the tobacco smoke at that singer in blue as he calmly replied, "I could tell you tales of hired guns sent to do a job on this child, but I was brung up to act modest. So let's just say I mean to get the son of a bitch who murdered Lorena Webber, and if the shoe don't fit, none of you need worry, or vice versa.''

Johnny Ringo didn't answer for a long time as the gal in the stage in blue sang a flirty tune about a Moor in French. When he had himself back under control, the well-educated professional tough's face was an odd mottled shade of flush and pallor as he stammered aloud, "Eight, nine, ten, and it just ain't working!" Then he turned on one high heel to stride off through the crowd before he could blow up in violation of Old Man Clanton's orders.

He didn't have to tell Longarm this. Longarm had been *trying* to get the mean bastard to blow up. A lawman wasn't allowed to just swat men like Johnny Ringo as if they were flies, but *somebody* was going to have to swat a hard case who killed men for refusing to drink with him!

Longarm started to order another whiskey, but settled for more draft beer. The only thing more contemptable than a mean drunk was a man who drank himself mean while thinking about mean drunks. He was starting to see what wise old Aggie Phillips had meant, in bed up in Saguaro Wells, when she'd warned him he could be biting off more than he could chew down this way. Like Miss Alice had said in that book about Wonderland, things seemed to be getting curiouser and curiouser as looking for the answer to one question only seemed to inspire *another* question!

Since that singer in blue across the saloon seemed the least of his worries, Longarm suddenly realized where he'd seen her before. It had been out California way, the time he'd shot it out with another killer in that Pueblo de Los Angeles opera house, while the opera was going on. When he'd dropped the villain center stage, he'd gotten a standing ovation and an invitation to ride east with the prima donna in her Pullman compartment. He'd enjoyed the trip a lot, but he'd seen too late that the one singing in Tombstone at the moment, the prima donna's understudy, had been younger and better-looking.

Longarm wondered what she could be doing in Tombstone, singing an aria all alone for a rougher crowd than she usually sang for. Then he put down his glass and turned away from the stage and the bar, muttering, "Skirt-chasing asshole!" as he headed for the door. For all he needed then and there was another ball to juggle as he tried to make a lick of sense from all the balls he had in the air.

It didn't *matter* what that young soprano from that opera company might be doing alone in Tombstone, if she was really alone. He'd seen she'd changed her hair color from brown to a sort of strawberry blond. As he headed back to his hotel, he wondered which color was natural to her and who might be keeping her if she wasn't in town alone.

He decided a gal being kept in a boomtown wouldn't be singing for her supper in a saloon. But that didn't mean she couldn't be keeping some worthless tenor with a big dick and a drinking problem.

He was laughing to himself as he entered the Cosmopolitan and went upstairs to his hired room next to the baths. His precautionary match stem was in place, and when he went into the room he found it was cool indoors by that hour. So he treated himself to a tub soak and got to bed earlier than usual, stretching out across the generous mattress as he mentally invited that strawberry blonde in blue to join him for the night so he could make it up to her for that big mistake aboard a Pullman car.

He couldn't get her to join him, of course, and even as he pictured her there, shaking her strawberry-blond head with an amused expression, he knew what he was doing. He was keeping his weary head from whirling like a top from worry to worry by concentrating on something worth thinking about that didn't really matter.

So the next thing Longarm knew, a teamster's whip was cracking down on Fremont Street and the bright sunlight told him he'd slept through better than eight hours like a log. As he lay there staring up at the pressed-tin ceiling, he realized he was hungry as a bitch wolf, but as bright-eyed and bushy-tailed as he'd ever want to feel. So he grinned and said, ''Good morning, ma'am, and I thank you for such a peaceful night for a change. But now that you've restored my strength and I seem to have a piss hard-on, I'd best get up and get cracking if I aim to crack this case!''

Chapter 11

John P. Clum of the *Tombstone Epitaph* was a dapper young man for all the wonders and cucumbers he'd crowded into less than thirty years so far. He and Longarm went back to when the both of them had been trying to put some members of the Indian Ring, left over from the Grant Administration, in jail.

A lawyer by training, John Clum had replaced the famous Overland coach manager, Tom Jeffords, as agent to the Chiricahuas back in '77, at the tender age of twenty-six, when the red-bearded blood brother to Cochise had resigned in disgust.

Clum hadn't lasted much longer. He'd never managed to get as close to his Apache wards as the man they'd called Taglito. But Clum had tried to be as fair as Jeffords, arguing for tribal police instead of cavalry troopers to keep the hotter heads in line, and helping a lot when Longarm had been sent to look into those reports of Indian allotments being sold in Tucson. He'd gotten no further with the BIA than Jeffords had. So, accused of being too soft by the whites and too hard-assed by the Indians, he'd resigned in turn to look for some other line of work.

He'd wound up running a job-printing shop and followed the boom to Tombstone with his gallies and press in a Conestaga wagon to publish his famous *Epitaph* to go with Ed Schieffelin's imaginary tombstone. He was sticking type in the back that morning when Longarm strode in to tell the pretty gal at the business counter that he didn't want to place an ad or report a dogfight.

When the owner in the back saw who it was, he set aside his typesetting stick and invited Longarm into his smaller private office for a sit-down by his rolltop desk. As he produced a pint from the desk, Clum asked, "Do you want to buy a newspaper cheap? It's way cooler out in Frisco, the Buckley Machine running things around the Frisco Bay isn't half as murderous, and I have the wife and a new baby daughter to consider."

Longarm sat down beside him to accept the heroic tumbler of redeye as he replied, "Heard you'd stopped screwing squaws and married up like a Christian. Congratulations on the kid, and how private a conversation can a lawman on a confidential side trip have with you, John?"

Clum blinked, laughed, and replied, "For Pete's sake, this is a *newspaper* office, pard! We publish all the news that's fit to print, and when there isn't enough of that to cast copy, we blank out the dirty words and let her rip. But keep talking. We might be able to work something out for an exclusive."

Longarm said, "That was what I had in mind. I need some information from someone in these parts with an ear to the ground. There might be some political corruption to the puzzle, and I hardly need to tell a Tombstone newspaper man why *that* thought occurred to me. On the other hand, it might turn out to be a simple flimflam forgery or even the vapors of a nervous bride."

Longarm knew he'd come to the right source when John Clum nodded and said, "You're talking about the marital troubles of Lester Twill and that Pima breed he married."

Longarm replied, "If he really married her. I heard different. I take it you're on his side?"

The newspaper man shook his head and said, "Let's not

get sickening. From the little I really know about either party, Lester Twill would be a knockaround prospector who's never had much luck, and the breed he married, a Clio something, was left some scattered holdings by a white prospecting dad who'd done one hell of a lot of walking for the few patches of color he ever found.''

Clum leaned back in his swivel chair to continue. "The wedding and their noisy wedding night took place here in town. Miss Clio had just bought a town house on Sixth Street after moving here from Yuma. She sent her Pima housemaid to fetch the law around midnight on a Saturday. Marshal White was home in bed. His deputy on duty, Virgil Earp, sent some boys over to Sixth Street to see what the fuss was about. They found her half naked and distraught, accusing Lester Twill of rape. They found the accused playing cards at the Oriental. So when he produced a fresh wedding certificate, they returned empty-handed for further instructions. Deputy Earp decided it might be best if Twill moved back to his boardinghouse while the couple's lawyers sorted things out. That's where things stood, the last I heard. We didn't run the story. One or the other has to be fibbing, and I can't afford to get get sued over third-page gossip.''

Longarm asked if Clum had made any attempt to verify the testimony of either party.

Clum shook his head and asked, "Why should I? Who *cares* if a half-ass prospector and his unpleasantly plump breed bride are happily or unhappily married?''

Longarm answered simply, "I do. Clio Hendersen sent her best white friend to me for help, swearing Lester Twill was out to jump a silver claim her daddy had left her. You say she's fat as well as desperate?''

Clum shrugged and said, "I may be spoiled. *My* lady is a looker. But this other lady we're talking about is part Pima, and as soon as Pima get off their usual diet of cactus fruit and rabbit meat, they tend to blow up like balloons. I've only seen this Clio around town a few times. I have to say she's too fat for me. But they say love conquers all.''

"Especially when the object of one's desire owns a silver mine,'' said Longarm dryly. He sipped the last of his whiskey, and asked if Clum knew anyone who'd been to the wedding.

The dapper newspaperman refreshed Longarm's shot glass as he replied in an off-hand tone, "Why should I? It was hardly the social event of the season. The way I heard, it was a civil service performed by a justice of the peace. Don't ask me which one. But I can find out.''

Longarm said, "I'd be obliged, when you have time. Got other fish to fry this morning. Starting with the mortal remains of Lorena Webber. I was told the Pima riding with her would bring her remains on into Tombstone.''

Clum nodded and said, "They did. We ran her murder in this morning's edition. I'll give you a copy on your way out. You'll see the deputy coroner, Doc Ryan, has slated his inquest for this afternoon. They'll want a statement from you if you tell them you're in town and spoke with the victim just before she was victimized.''

Longarm put his shot glass on the edge of the desk and placed a hand over it in polite refusal as he said, "I'll cross that bridge when I get to it. It's early enough to make some more important calls this side of La Siesta. It's her talking to me up in Saguaro Wells that has me half convinced about that otherwise simple domestic dispute. If we buy Lester Twill's tale that he married Clio Hendersen out of the goodness of his heart . . .''

"He did. Right here in town. In front of witnesses,'' Clum declared.

Longarm said, "I wish you'd let your elders finish before sounding off. Miss Lorena told me she'd been to Tucson to check with the county clerk and and compare signatures on their copy. They told her that as far as anyone could tell, her old school chum had married Lester Twill fair and square, then accused him of rape when he exercised his rights as a lawful husband. On the face of it, she was just being silly.''

"Then what's the problem?'' asked the newspaperman.

Longarm said, ''The problem is that Lorena Webber is dead and that somebody tried to do me the same favor right after she'd come to me to tell me Lester Twill was a deep-dyed villain who'd somehow sold everyone but her poor pal Clio that he'd married the owner of that silver mine in Chindi Canyon.''

Clum frowned thoughtfully and said, ''I follow your drift. Neither Twill nor anyone in cahoots with him would have any reasons to kill the innocent friend of a hysterical wife. Knowing his legal records would stand up in any court, and knowing his wife was already telling anyone who'd listen that she'd never married him, he should have been willing to let one more woman accuse him on hearsay evidence all she might have wanted! So the murder of Lorena Webber does cast sinister shadows on the self-proclaimed bridegroom, doesn't it!''

"To a point.'' Longarm sighed, reaching for a cheroot as he went on. ''Miss Lorena told me she was in the beef business out this way. Last night Old Man Clanton sent Johnny Ringo to express a paternal interest in the little lady's herd. I don't know how many cows she owned the night she died. But even a modest herd might tempt many a hardcase with the price of beef higher this year than last.''

Clum whistled softly and said, ''You *did* come to the right place. We just stuck her obit, so some of the figures are fresh in my mind. The late Lorena Webber was divorced and unspoken for. So the six or eight hundred head she's been grazing over in the foothills of the Dragoons will doubtless be probated to her kin back in Texas. I understand she has a married sister in San Antone. They tell me she stayed with her part-Pima schoolmate or over at the Exchange Hotel whenever she rode in from her own spread, the Running W, out past Antelope Springs a hard hour's ride to the northeast.''

Longarm lit his cheroot and shook out the match before he mused, "I've ridden that range. The Clanton spread at Lewis Springs ain't far enough away to matter. Your turn."

Clum grimaced and decided, "If Old Man Clanton and his boys put their four heads together, it might add up to a half-wit. To call them white trash would be to flatter them, and Johnny Ringo is worse. The Clantons were born stupid and vicious. Johnny Ringo née Rhinegold is an educated man from a wealthy family who's *chosen* to be a miserable two-gun tough. But old N. H. Clanton has a certain wolverine cunning to go with his sticky fingers, and I can't see why he'd want to start up with a federal lawman a good two days ride away if all he wanted was Lorena Webber's herd."

Longarm said, "I keep getting stuck on that same sandbar. Who'd be tending that Running W herd now, with its owner lying dead here in town?"

Clum said, "I heard she has an Anglo ramrod, a Chinese cook, and a handful of *vaqueros* and their *mujeres* out by Antelope Springs. Why do you ask?"

Longarm said, "It would have made more sense for the Clantons to go after *them* than *me*. I'm missing something. I got more suspects with half-baked motives than I can use. I got to narrow things down if I expect to make much sense of this compost heap in the time I have to fork it over. I can't talk to Clio Hendersen or Clanton if neither are in town this morning. You say Lester Twill is staying in some lodging house here in Tombstone?"

Clum set his glass aside and rose from his desk as he nodded and replied, "Cam Fly's lodging house. I can point it out from my front door."

So Longarm got rid of his own glass and rose to follow the newspaperman out front. As they passed through the press room, Clum gave him a copy of that morning's edition. As they stood in the doorway, Clum pointed out a strip of sunlight spilling through the facades on the south side of Fremont and said, "That one-story 'dobe is the assay office Twill works in. He boards in that two-story frame across that empty lot from it. Cam Fly runs a photograph gallery on the ground floor and offers lodgings up above it."

Rolling up the free newspaper, Longarm agreed the mining man ought to be one place or the other, and said he was much obliged.

Clum said, "Don't mention it, but watch yourself. Fly charges dear and caters to a crowd who's been thrown out of more respectable places."

Longarm said, "That's all right. I've been thrown out of lots of respectable places my ownself. I'll see you later."

Clum softly murmured, "We hope," as Longarm crossed to the shadier side, slapping the rolled-up newspaper against his leg as if it were a riding crop.

He passed Bauer's meat market and turned into the smaller assay office. An older man wearing a blue eyeshade as he messed with acid and ore samples told him Lester Twill had quit. He added, "The kid married a Pima squaw who owns a silver mine. Ain't that a bitch?"

Longarm thanked him and stepped back outside. He crossed the sunbaked vacant lot, trampled dusty-bare by ponies crossing it to the rear entrance of that O.K. Corral fronting on Allan Street, to try Fly's lodging house on the far side.

A sad-eyed old cuss mopping the vestibule said Lester Twill didn't stay there anymore. When Longarm asked if Twill had left a forwarding address, the swamper said he'd ask.

He came back a million years later with a younger man in shirtsleeves under a black vest and rubber apron. That one said he ran the lodging house and the photographic business in the back. When he demanded some identification, Longarm produced his wallet and federal badge as he explained, "I am anxious to question Lester Twill about a possible federal case, Mr. Fly. Seeing I can't question him here, I've been hoping somebody might be able to tell me where I might.''

Camillus Fly shrugged and said, "It's no skin off my nose. I don't have the house number, but you're looking for a frame cottage painted spinach with tomato trim near the corner of Sixth and Allan. He said he was moving in with his new bride. We heard she's a fat breed. But that's his misfortune and none of our own.''

Longarm blinked in surprise and asked, "He's back at the town house of Clio Hendersen? I was told he'd been ordered by the Tombstone law not to darken her door again before they sorted out their confusing domestic situation.''

Camillus Fly calmly replied, "I heard about that. I just said it was no skin off my nose. I asked the squirt about what Marshal White had advised as he was packing up to go. Twill told me his own lawyer said the advice of a town marshal didn't carry the weight of a court order. Also, his wife had gone home to her mother and somebody had to watch the house the two of them held title to.''

Fly added, "If the truth be known, I suspect Lester was just out to save money by moving out before his next week's rent came due. For a mining man who bragged so much, he was sort of cheap.''

Longarm nodded as if he knew, and asked if they might be talking about a rat-faced cuss called Lawyer Trevor.

When Fly confessed he'd never asked, Longarm said, "That's all right. I'll ask myself. Sixth and Allan, right?''

Camillus Fly replied, "Right on the edge of the whore-house district. You can't miss it. Any place that isn't a private residence over on Sixth Street will have whores hanging out the front windows. Marshal White doesn't allow them to sell themselves out on the walks.''

Chapter 12

Tombstone was compact enough to get around on foot. But as he legged it up the slope to Sixth Street, keeping time with his rolled-up copy of the *Epitaph,* Longarm was starting to regret his frock coat with the sun rising higher. When he got to Fremont and Sixth, he turned to his right. His doing this inspired more than one soiled dove to rush to her window in various states of *deshabille*. For though the going fine for soliciting on the street was twenty dollars, there was nothing on the books about bare tits on a windowsill.

From earlier visits and the droll columns of the very paper he was smacking against his leg along the way, Longarm knew the painted and gussied-up gals leering and jeering at him from both sides of Sixth Street on a slow workday bore handles such as Snake Hips Sue, Dutch Annie, Mex Martha, Greek Gloria, or Frenching Flo. Few of them were really good-looking, and he knew the best-looking whores would be the most stupid. Ugly gals went into whoring because they had no choice no matter how smart they were. A good-looking gal who put out three ways for three dollars in a world so filled with rich and lonely men was simply dumb or out to punish herself, for some loco reason.

A gal who wasn't bad-looking called out in an intelligent tone that she'd spend the coming siesta with him for two dollars. Longarm idly wondered how she'd gotten herself so scrambled as he ticked his hat brim politely and called back that he had to meet another lady.

At a tamale stand near the corner of Sixth and Allan, Longarm asked directions, and crossed over to a spinach house with tomato trim as he ate a tamale with one hand and beat time with the *Epitaph* with the other. He dallied out front long enough to down the snack, and then he stepped up on the porch to twist the brass doorbell.

After some time a fat and shy Indian woman of around fifty came to the door in a print Mother Hubbard to tell him they didn't want any. Longarm flashed his federal badge and told her he'd been told he might find either Lester Twill or the proper owner of the house, Clio Hendersen, there.

Their housekeeper, if that was who she was, told Longarm he'd come to the wrong place. When he insisted, she allowed she worked for Clio Hendersen, or had, but hadn't seen her for some time. She said she thought her boss lady was visiting with other Indians off in the cactus somewhere. He hadn't been able to get Little Eva or Topsy to tell him where that Pima village might be either.

When he repeated his question about Lester Twill, she said he'd heard wrong about that. She said Miss Clio had left orders that the Saltu who claimed to be her man was not to set foot in her house for any reason. When Longarm asked if he might come in out of the noonday sun while they talked some more about the situation, she shook her head and told him she only worked there and had no orders about *him*. So he told her where he might be found if ever her boss lady came on home. Then he raced high noon back to the Cosmopolitan Hotel with his coat off over his left arm.

He'd naturally kept the room key on him. But the clerk

hailed him from the desk to say a lady had just been there looking for him.

Longarm stepped over to the desk to ask in a quieter tone whether they were talking about a rather large lady with some Indian blood that might show.

The clerk shook his head and replied, "White as you or me, but way better-looking. Had on a summer frock of light ecru and wore her straw boater on a crest of strawberry-blond curls. Said her name was Lamont. Madame-Mo-Zell Marie Lamont. Ain't that a mouthful?"

Longarm said, "I suspect she must have spotted me in the crowd at the Crystal Palace last night. We once toured with the same opera company. Did she say where she was staying here in Tombstone?"

The clerk shook his balding head and replied, "I never asked. She said she'd be back later."

So when Longarm went up to his room, he sponged under his arms and splashed some bay rum from a saddlebag over his hot hide before he put his shirt back on. Had things been different, he'd have stripped to the buff and flopped atop the covers bare-ass. For by now it was no-shit-ninety-or-more *indoors* as the ferocious Arizona sun cleared the streets of Tombstone for a spell.

Longarm knew Marie Lamont wasn't about to return until after the heat broke around three-thirty or four. Just as he knew that the one sure way to have a woman catch you bare-ass would be to take off your duds because she wasn't coming. He thought back to that midnight in Cheyenne, when he'd been alone in a hired room much like this one, squatting on the chamber pot as naked as a jay, to have the door he'd thought he'd locked swing suddenly open as he was letting go with a ripping fart.

The hell of it was, he would never know just what the woman he saw standing there in his open doorway, outlined by the hall light, had really looked like. Young or old, ugly or pretty, but surely a woman because of the lamplight on long hair and the girlish gasp she'd given as she crawfished

97

back and slammed the door shut again. Longarm would never know who she'd been, what she'd been expecting as she opened a door to catch a naked man shitting, or worse yet, whether she'd been one of the other hotel guests in the dining room the next morning.

If she had, and she'd recognized him with his clothes on, she'd have made a fine poker player. He'd known there was nothing *he* could do at breakfast but eat his damned waffles poker-faced.

Hence, on this later occasion, Longarm spread his free copy of the *Epitaph* across the bedcovers to recline beside them, reading up on current events in Tombstone.

John Clum had covered Lorena Webber's death politely but sort of tersely in his "Death's Doings" column. He'd reported Lorena hailed from a fine old Texas cattle clan and that Sheriff Charles Shibell was investigating her murder. The only other gunshot victim in the column was a Chinese mining man called Freddy Fong who'd been gunned by the "protector" of a white woman the late Freddy Fong had asked for a crime against nature. Clum had dryly added that the deputy coroner was treating this as a simple case of suicide.

Longarm read on, trying to get the feel of the small tough town's current pulse. He'd already noticed it was an election year. Tombstone Township was hoping they'd win the right to elect their own county officials. One of the owners of the Dexter Corral, the dapper John Behan, had announced he was willing to serve as sheriff. John Clum editorialized against such a notion, pointing out that a livery man had a vested interest in the comings and goings of cowboys.

Cowboy had started out back East as a polite term for a stock thief, and many a merchant and mining man still used the term in its original sense.

The love-hate relationships of the residents of Tombstone and their more rustic neighbors all around reminded Longarm of some unhappily married couple with nobody else they could screw. It was easy to see why mining men and cowhands irritated one another. Mining men tended to be older and more settled down, with wives and daughters to worry about as they drew thrice the pay for steadier work. Cowhands tended to be young if they still enjoyed their chores, and considered mining men overpaid spoilsports when the outfit rode in on a payday night to let off a little steam. The businessmen who charged dearly for helping such lads let off such steam had to balance the profits and losses of such transient trade, and tended to divide along the lines charged in the *Epitaph*: political hacks, backed by blacksmiths, corral owners, saddle shops, and such, against the butchers, bakers, and yep, candle-stick makers who catered to the more thrifty but more prosperous hardrock mining men and their families.

Neither side could get along without the other because ten thousand souls ate a stupendous amount of fresh meat and produce, while the country folk all around needed someplace to market it. Stuck as it was in the Sonora Desert, Tombstone depended for fresh food on the scattered but productive irrigated truck farms of desert-wise Mexican and some Pima farmers. Most of the hog raisers taking care of Tombstone's kitchen waste and worse were Anglo, set up closer to town. A lot of poultry and eggs were produced smack *in* most towns of the times. Fresh beef, along with veal or lamb, which was usually goat in Arizona Territory, was grazed further out, mostly along the greener slopes of the Dragoons to the east or Mule Mountains to the west. So both sides were better off because of one another, and this naturally drove a lot of mean drunks *loco en la cabeza* when they thought about it. Setting Tombstone up as a county seat for the mostly Republican businessmen and mostly Democrat cattlemen to squabble over would mean they could have some noisy times in the near future. Another John named John H. Slaughter was suggested by John Clum as a compromise the cow and silver barons might consider, if only *he* could be persuaded to run for sheriff.

For the thirty-nine-year-old ex–Texas Ranger was a happily married man of substance, with one hell of a herd he'd come by honestly.

The upright but sort of short John H. had declined the offer from the Tombstone Democrats for now, saying he was too busy with his new ranch near the border, with Victorio on the warpath that summer. So Clum had picked Virgil Earp as the Republican lesser of two evils, predicting the Fall of Rome, at least, if ever Johnny Behan became sheriff of their proposed Cochise County. The idealistic John Clum didn't seem to worry about party lines as much as he worried about law and order.

Longarm hoped he knew what he was doing. He'd heard conflicting gossip about Deputy Town Marshal Virgil Earp and his tagalong kid brothers. Longarm wanted to talk to Earp about that rape or wedding night misunderstanding he'd handled as Marshal White's night ramrod in any case. He'd heard Virgil Earp owned shares in a silver mine. He'd heard he owned shares in a whorehouse. You heard things like that when half a community seemed at feud with the other half.

Longarm looked up from his reading as a sudden roll of thunder rumbled across the sky outside. He rose and went to the window to open the blinds. It wasn't raining outside. Two days of rain in a row would be asking too much of the thunderbird on the Sonora. But the sky above was overcast as distant lightning flickered off to the south, and when he opened the sash it felt way cooler than it should have that afternoon. So he left it open for such breezes as there might be to blow freely, and lit a fresh smoke as he stood there to cool off.

So he was feeling friskier than he might have at that hour when there came a tapping on the door. Longarm strode over to it with the cheroot gripped in his expectant grin, but drew his .44-40 in passing the bedpost just in case.

When he flung the door open with his six-gun pointed polite but handy, Longarm saw that, as he'd hoped, the strawberry-blond Marie Lamont was the one standing there in the hall with a radiant smile. It was one hell of an improvement over that gal in Cheyenne who'd caught him on the chamber pot. So he put the six-gun and cheroot to one side as he hauled her in and kissed her friendly while he kicked the door shut behind her.

Her body felt friendly under the thin ecru silk she had on as she started to kiss back, then stiffened and shoved him away, demanding, "Are you out of your mind? What sort of a woman do you take me for?"

Longarm let go, and made sure he'd really hit the ashtray on the dresser by the door with that lit cheroot while he soberly assured her he'd been trying to greet her as the old pal he considered her.

The soprano he recalled in a more revealing stage outfit smiled some more despite herself and said, "I fear you have me confounded with the prima donna you spent all that time with aboard our Pullman car, Deputy Long. I was her understudy. *She* was the one who was under you most of the time."

Longarm waved her to a seat as he calmly replied, "My friends call me Custis, and were you peeking through keyholes, Miss Marie? What I may or may not have done in private with another lady is none of your beeswax, no offense. How would you like it if someone was to accuse *you* of being under me most of the time?"

Marie Lamont grimaced and replied, "Never mind. I'm here because I heard you were in town, I do remember you from that time out on the West Coast, and I need to make some money!"

Longarm had noticed she'd taken a seat on a bentwood chair near the foot of the bed instead of the way he'd been waving. So he waved at the bed again as he said, "Well, I hardly ever pay. But seeing you have such a swell figure and seeing you seem desperate, we might be able to work something out just this once."

"Asshole!" she almost screamed. "I wouldn't let you

101

touch me if you were the last man on earth!''

Longarm picked up the six-gun from the dresser and moved over to slide it back in his holster on the bedpost as he quietly suggested, ''I doubt I'd have to be the last man on earth. A desert island would likely change your mind after we'd been stuck there no more than ten years. I take it you've come to sell me something other than your fair white body?''

She repressed a shudder and replied, ''You've certainly got *that* right! How could you have gone all the way with that dreadful ancient crone? She was overweight and over thirty and it just wasn't fair that she never missed a damned performance so *I* could go on!''

Longarm sat on the bed to face her as he said, ''I was wondering why you were singing in that saloon last night. Did you quit or get fired, Miss Marie?''

She sighed, shrugged, and replied, ''I suppose it was mutual. Did you really . . . you know . . . more than three times in a row the way that silly old cow boasted about you later?''

Longarm answered simply, ''I'm a man, and she wasn't half as old and fat as you suggest. Could we get to what it was you came here to sell me, if that wasn't it?''

She said, ''I know another man, a more respectable man with a large amount of money to invest.''

Longarm dryly asked, ''How much are you asking from *him* then?''

The soprano snapped, ''Don't be beastly. If I *was* a whore, I wouldn't be singing in a saloon and neither of you could hope to meet my price.''

She struck a pose to add, ''I've always thought that if ever I did sell my favors to any man, it would have to be somebody as grand as the Prince of Wales. More than one swain has remarked on my resemblance to Miss Lily Langtry, when she was younger, and they say the Prince of Wales kept her in a stately London mansion with a staff of servants and all.''

Longarm scowled and said, "*Bueno,* you're just too high-toned by half for even that rich dude with all that money to invest. Who is he and what does he want to invest in?"

The self-important soprano said, "Silver, of course. Why else would anyone from Boston Town be out here shopping for his own silver mine? I'm required to, ah, *mingle* after the show at the Crystal Palace. I've yet to let even one of those big spenders *kiss* me. But I have to *chat,* and when Mr. Wentworth heard I knew you, he got all excited and said he'd make it worth my while if I could set up a meeting between the two of you. So what about it?"

Longarm frowned thoughtfully and said, "That's easy enough to work out. But how come? Where did your Mr. Wentworth get the notion this child, a U.S. deputy marshal, might have a silver mine to sell him?"

She demurely replied, "I don't know. Why don't we ask him while we have supper with him this evening?"

Chapter 13

She didn't know where. The mysterious Boston dude had said he'd send a carriage to her hotel for her around sundown because he dined at eight, the way rich folks liked to. She told Longarm she was staying at the Grand Hotel. That figured, and it wasn't too far for him to walk. So they agreed to meet in her lobby around sundown. He rose, but didn't even try to kiss her hand as she flounced out.

He went downstairs to buy a copy of the *Tombstone Nugget* at the newsstand in his own lobby. That gave him something else to read as he waited out the siesta, which ran shorter in Tombstone than most towns that close to the border because so many of the folks there were new to the Southwest and it never got too hot down in a hardrock mine in any case.

There was nothing in the rival *Nugget* about him. They'd run the story about a local cattle gal getting shot in the head as a possible Apache atrocity. The *Nugget* didn't admire any Indians half as much as the former BIA man putting out the *Epitaph*. Longarm hadn't even considered Victorio and his Bronco Apache as Lorena Webber's killers. To begin with she'd been riding with Pima, and no Nadéné with a lick of sense would aim at a white gal and leave her Pima escort alive.

By now it was after three and when he tried again, things were open again along Fremont Street. So he went to the Western Union to wire Denver and Saguaro Wells, letting his home office and the lawmen who were holding his prisoner know where he was. Then he ambled on to see John Clum at the *Epitaph* again.

Clum came out from the back with an envelope in hand, and suggested they take it on over to the Capital Saloon because Clum was meeting a cowboy there with a story to sell. When pals saw you going into a newspaper office, they might suspect you were selling stories about *them*.

As they strode east along Fremont together, Clum handed Longarm the envelope, saying, "You'll find the names of the JP and the wedding party witnesses you asked about in there. It wasn't tough. Lester Twill and Clio Hendersen were married in the JP's parlor just after suppertime, and the witnesses were the neighbors who'd been rocking on the porch and had nothing better to do. The blushing bride called the law on him the same night. I frankly don't see much of a story there. A knockaround mining man talks a fat rich breed into a hasty wedding, and as they sober up she changes her mind. Whether she knew what she was doing or sincerely didn't remember marrying a poor boy suspected of Lord knows what, I don't see any mystery here."

Longarm said, "I do. When I went over to Clio Hendersen's, I was told neither were there and I couldn't come in. Yet Cam Fly had told me Lester Twill had been staying there. Don't you find that sort of mysterious?"

Clum frowned thoughtfully and replied, "I find it dumb, at least. Fred White's an easygoing lawman, but he is the law and he did tell Lester Twill to stay away from that particular address."

Longarm said, "He's got to be staying somewhere. Clio Hendersen is out of town and they won't let me inside her town house."

Clum whistled and said, "I follow your drift! He'd be

risking a pistol-whipping from Fred White or worse from his estranged wife's Indian relatives if she came home to find him there. So he must not be expecting her to come home and find him there!''

Longarm asked, ''Why do you reckon either one of 'em would want to live on Sixth Street, with all those untidy neighbors hanging their tits out their windows, seeing she's supposed to be both rich and more respectable?''

The man who lived in Tombstone said, ''That's easy. She's a breed. If she was purebred or Mex, she'd have trouble getting a place as far west as Sixth. Mexicans, Indians, and the few colored families we have in Tombstone tend to string out along Seventh, on the downwind edge of town. The only non-whites west of Sixth in any numbers are the few Chinese of Hoptown, a little over one square block cut off from Third Street by the Mountain Maid mining layout. You say she has a full-blood keeping house for her? There you go. The whores on her block are probably complaining about her undesirable visitors. Where do you suspect Lester Twill hid the body?''

Longarm said, ''Too early to say. The Pima I rode in with told me they were expecting to meet up with Miss Clio in their own private quarters. They call her Porevo, whatever that means.''

The former Indian agent said, ''It means She-Chief in Pima. So they must think more highly of her than the real-estate agents here in town. Her tribal title makes my point that something must've happened to her and Lester Twill must know about it!''

Longarm put the envelope away, saying, ''I'll scout up these other folks who may or may not back his claim he married her fair and square before she decided she didn't like him. I doubt I'll have time this evening.''

Crum asked if he'd be attending that inquest into the killing of Lorena Webber.

Longarm said, ''Nobody's invited me and I wasn't there. I sure mean to read the findings of your deputy coroner's jury. But I have no light to shed on any death by rifle fire, and if I did, I'd still be too busy.''

As they approached the Capitol Saloon on the corner of Fremont and Fourth, Longarm asked, ''What can you tell me about a gent from Boston Town who calls himself Wentworth and claims to be interested in the silver lodes in these parts?''

The man who published a paper in a silver mining town looked sort of surprised as he replied, ''L. J. Wentworth, Boston's answer to old Meyer Guggenheim? I didn't know he was down this way, and you can't ask me to sit on *this* story, Custis!''

''Sit on what?'' asked Longarm. ''I'd be obliged if you'd hold off until after I've had supper with the cuss this evening. I'd be proud to give you one of them exclusives if you'd give me time to find out what he wants!''

John Clum said, ''In a word, and as you suggested, silver. Old L. J. Wentworth is a major shareholder in the Comstock Lode and mines his own scattered lodes clean across the Great Basin. I've said from the beginning that Tombstone was going to rival Virginia City before we bottomed out down this way! L. J. Wentworth wouldn't be in town if he wasn't on to something, and you say you're having supper with him?''

Longarm said, ''Me and an opera-singing gal. I'm still working on how come. I don't have any silver stock to sell. The only silver I've heard much about in these parts would be that unproven lode that Miss Clio Hendersen's daddy left her over in Chindi Canyon.''

They strode inside and bellied up to the bar as Clum told him he'd heard the last word about that claim. ''Silver sulfide, assaying out to fifteen to twenty a ton. Not quite as rich as Ed Schieffelin's first big strike over this way, but nothing to be sneezed at. Men have shot it out over less than five-a-ton ore.''

''Would less than the highest-grade sulfide be worth it to a big silver baron such as this L. J. Wentworth?'' Longarm asked. "I met a poor jasper up Utah way one time trying to unload a proven gold mine, cheap, because it was medium-grade color way the hell up a dry canyon. Nobody was buying because it would have cost more to lay rails and water pipes that far than all the gold in the canyon would have been worth."

Clum caught the barkeep's eye and signaled for two of his usuals as he told Longarm, "We're still shipping stamped-and-washed high-grade by freight wagon and showing a healthy profit that you can see all around. Fuel for a smelter would be a problem over in the Dragoons, but with a wood-fired stamping mill, you could upgrade ten-a-ton enough to pay its way to the railroad less than eighty miles off. Wentworth must have heard you were mixed up in Clio Hendersen's domestic dispute with a suspected claim jumper. He probably wants you to tell him which of two tall stories to believe."

The barkeep slid two bourbons with beer chasers across the mahogany to them. So they clinked and drank to hysterical women and no-luck prospectors willing to marry them, or claim they had, which was even sillier.

Clum opined, and Longarm had to agree, that if Lester Twill was lying, he had balls cast from high-carbon steel.

When the newspaperman said something about waiting for that lone cowhand with a tale to tell about a gang of cow thieves, Longarm lit out for the Grand Hotel, and got there before Marie Lamont had come down from her room. He didn't care. He found a club chair where a man could smoke and read the *Scientific American* magazine while he waited for her. Like many self-educated men, Longarm liked to read right to the edges of his current understanding. Some of the articles in the magazine passed clean over his head, but he memorized some new words to look up, and there was an article on ballistics he found interesting as all hell.

Marie Lamont came down from her room in her own good time, dressed for dining at eight in a frock of blue sateen with a Spanish comb and white lace *mantilla* instead of her straw boater.

When Longarm set his magazine aside and rose to greet her, she told him to put out that filthy cigar.

He waved her to the club chair beside his own as he politely but firmly replied, "If this was your parlor instead of a public lobby, I might overlook your tone and obey your royal command. But it ain't, and if you don't like my company I'll just be on my way."

She sat down, saying, "You can't leave now. Mr. Wentworth is sending his carriage for us any minute."

So he sat down, the cheroot still gripped between his teeth as he put his hat back on and said, "I heard a tad more about this Boston boy of yours since last we met, Miss Marie. They say he's a genuine silver baron. Is he paying for you turning up late for work at that saloon this evening?"

She made a wry face and declared, "He's paying me for a night's work, with tips figured in. I told you I was only doing this for the money. What time is it?"

He replied without reaching for the watch in his vest pocket that they had some time to bicker before sundown at the rate the fool sun was setting.

Then, as if to make a liar of him, a young squirt dressed sort of like an English coachman off a tea tin came in to ask if they were the ones Mr. Wentworth was expecting for supper.

Longam allowed they were, and rose to help the strawberry blonde in blue to her feet. They went outside to find an open carriage drawn by four black horses waiting at the curb. Their driver helped them both in, and climbed up his own seat to crack his whip and get them all started to the west, into the last rays of a glorious desert sunset, as Marie described it.

Longarm stared out idly as they crossed Third Street and swung south to avoid a confusion of steam-engine stacks and mine hoists outlined in black against the sky. Longarm asked their driver how far they had to go. He called back in a jolly tone that they were almost there, adding that his boss had rented a town house just to the south for the summer.

As if to show he meant it, he reined in just two blocks south to point with his whip at a massive structure looming sort of ominously against a now-blood-red western sky as he told them they'd arrived.

Longarm had climbed in last, so he dropped out to help Marie down before their driver could. The driver thanked him and said he'd run the carriage around to the back.

As Longarm escorted the strawberry blonde toward the big black front door of the house, she murmured, "This place looks more like a *warehouse* than the mansion of a silver baron!"

Longarm replied, "I noticed. The boy said they'd had to rent it. Maybe they have it gussied up fancier inside."

They didn't. Another figure in servant's livery opened the front door before Longarm could knock, and announced Mr. Wentworth had been expecting them. But when they stepped inside, they found that the entry opened on to a ballroom-sized expanse of woodblock paving, dimly lit from above. Marie stared up at the crimson sky above the roofless interior to gasp. "Good heavens, this *is* a deserted warehouse!"

Longarm was staring thoughtfully at the three men lined up along a lumber pile in front of four open archways through the back wall as he quietly replied, "Not quite deserted and still being built."

Then Marie recognized the tall portly one in the middle, laughed nervously, and called out, "Oh, *there* you are, Mr. Wentworth. Are we going somewhere else from here?"

The big soft-looking man she'd asked quietly replied, "No, my dear. You've brought the famous skirt-chasing Longarm right where we wanted him."

The door behind them slammed shut like the entrance to

111

a tomb as the one who'd lured them in chortled, "That's for damned sure!"

The four of them had shared the same mistake in watching Longarm's holstered six-gun under his frock coat. Three of them seemed to need orders to draw on the man they had boxed. Longarm didn't worry about what their portly leader was waiting for. He stiff-armed the soprano with his left hand, and crabbed the other way as he fired the double derringer he'd been palming in his *right* hand. So Marie and the lean and hungry gunhand with his holster tied down hit the blocks at the same time, one limp as a dishrag with a bullet in his brain and the other screaming fit to bust in high C.

Longarm landed on his right hip, and rolled to cover the one behind him just as that one fired. The doorkeeper's bullet whipped through the space where Longarm had been, to fold the pal facing their way like a gutshot jackknife. Before he could correct his aim, Longarm nailed him over the left eyebrow with a last derringer bullet, and let go of the spent belly gun to grab for his .44-40.

As the one he'd shot last went down, Longarm just had time to peg one wild six-gun shot at the one running out the back way, screaming almost as loud as the soprano down on the floor with Longarm. Then he was gone and as Longarm rose, smoking six-gun in hand and spent derringer dangling at the end of his watch chain, they heard a loud rattle of carriage wheels and pounding hooves. So Longarm circled the lumber pile and ran out into the gathering darkness to no avail. When he saw he was alone out back, he returned to the lady he'd knocked on her ass and put his hardware away to help her up. As he got her up on her feet, he dryly remarked, "That was dumb of me. But you sure don't *look* Mexican."

Chapter 14

Somewhere in the night an alarm triangle was clanging, and there were shouting voices even closer as Longarm led Marie to a corner with that lumber between them and the door, saying, "I doubt those last aspiring assassins will be back. But you just saw how it pays a body to suspect the worse."

She gasped, "My God! How did you know? And what was that about me looking Mexican?"

He chuckled fondly and replied, "You weren't listening. I said the opposite. The first time anyone tried to kill me that way, it was this pretty Mexican gal taking me home to meet her *mamacita* in Nuevo Laredo."

The strawberry blonde wailed, "Oh, no! You don't think they sent me to lure you into this death trap, do you!"

Longarm calmly replied, "Sure I do. They did. You just didn't know it. That one who said he was a famous mining man suckered you into an invite to supper, figuring I'd hardly suspect a pretty gal I already knew. I didn't and I don't. For all your faults, I remember you as an opera singer instead of a gunman's doxie, and it's safe to assume they meant to do you too."

"Oh, Dear Lord!" she wailed. "What have I gotten myself into?"

He assured her, "You're likely at least halfways *out*.

Like I said, they were using you to bait the hook. You don't worry much about the worm when the big one gets away, no offense. I know you could still point out that one who said he was L. J. Wentworth. He knows it too. But it makes way more sense for the two who got away to just keep going.''

''But who were they and how did you know who they really were?'' she demanded as the shouts out in the night grew nearer.

Longarm said, ''I don't know who they were. I figured they were up to something step by step. To begin with, I didn't have any silver to sell a silver baron. When I thought he might have wanted me to put him in touch with a lady who *does* have some silver to sell, I didn't see how anyone here in Tombstone could have known, *last night,* that I knew such a lady. I hadn't talked to anyone in Tombstone about her silver claim. I was talking to Johnny Ringo about a lady with *cows* to sell when you spotted me from the stage. I'd gone back to my hotel alone by the time you mentioned me to that fat boy you recalled as a silver baron because he was fibbing. How do you like it so far?''

She stared at him owl-eyed and marveled, ''I see what you mean. *He* was the one who said he wanted to talk to you about Arizona silver. I told him you were a famous lawman, and sort of fresh. He must have known all along that you knew that other woman who had silver to sell and . . . what does she look like?''

Longarm said, ''I've yet to lay eyes on her. I asked around town about your Mr. Wentworth, and outfoxed myself by having the real L. J. Wentworth described to me as an upright silver baron. But when that carriage commenced to take us to have supper with a silver baron on the unfashionable side of Tombstone's Chinatown, my suspicions were aroused some more, and as you see, I carry a double derringer at the other end of this watch chain. That Mexican gal they sent to lure me into a similar setup made the mistake of leading me into the dark deserted meat stalls behind

114

the Plaza del Toros on a weeknight, and I just couldn't see any *mamacita* dwelling there when the bullfights were not in progress."

He gazed around the expanse of the building under construction, now almost totally dark, as he added, "I knew as we stepped through yonder door that we were never going to be served supper here. Their mistake was taking the time to gloat before they sprang their trap."

A sliver of lantern light rent the blackness across the way as a cautious voice called in to them, "What was all that shooting about? I'd be Deputy Marshal Zeb Crabbe, and they tell me the gunshots came from somewhere around here."

Longarm called back, "They did. I'd be U.S. Deputy Custis Long, and I just had it out with five gunslicks I never saw before. Two of 'em got away."

The door opened wider, spilling lantern light as far as the corpse of the fake doorman. Then others packing lanterns crowded in to shed considerable literal light on the scene, even as Longarm was trying in vain to give a sensible account of why he and a famous opera singer in a spanking-new summer frock had expected to have supper with anyone in a warehouse under construction.

Then John Clum from the *Epitaph* showed up with his notebook to say he'd run out on his wife and babe for a headline and meant by the Great Horned Spoon to have one!

Longarm decided, "I reckon the other side already knows as much as I could hope to hide from you and your readers, and the two of us never got that supper we've been saving up for. So I'll make you a deal, John. If you can get us shed of this crowd in a sit-down place to eat as we talk, I'll give you that exclusive we talked about earlier."

Clum excused himself long enough to have a word with Marshal White in the flesh, who'd driven over from his own house across town, and in no time at all the four of them were sitting around a table in the Can-Can Restaurant on Fourth Street, near Longarm's hotel.

Longarm and the strawberry blonde ordered the specials. John Clum and Marshal White, having supped already, ordered coffee and cake. Longarm did most of the talking as they were waiting because John Clum was taking notes, Marie Lamont was still confused about what had happened, and the older Fred White never had much to say.

Unlike the town-taming Bear River Smith who'd pistol-whipped the town of Abilene into submission in forty-eight hours, and got hit in the head with an ax within months, or James Butler Hickok, who'd *failed* to tame Abilene and been fired, the quiet but amiable Marshal White tried to stay on the good side of the town and country factions that made Saturday nights in Tombstone so tense. His only comment for publication was that nobody he'd talked to in the crowd around those three fresh corpses had any notion who they might have been.

The newspaperman waited until Longarm said *he* had no idea who'd sent them, or why, before he sighed and said, "I wish somebody *famous* would get killed in Tombstone. The bigger papers across the country reprint tales of gunfights between shootists with reputations. But when I ran the shootout between our own John Slaughter and a cow thief called Gallagher, nobody cared."

"Who won?" asked Marie, wide-eyed.

As the waiter delivered their orders, the young newspaperman sighed and said, "John Slaughter, of course. But that's what I mean. Had the two of you been ambushed by, say, Buckskin Frank, Johnny Ringo, Curly Bill, and Doc Holliday, or all four of the Clanton Gang, we'd have the makings of a legend here. But I don't know what I can make out of a trio of unknown saddle tramps, Custis. What else have you got for me?"

As he and Marie dug in to their roast beef, mashed potatoes, and string beans later than either usually supped, Longarm tersely but truthfully brought John Clum and his

116

readers up to date on his reasons for riding down from Saguaro Wells while his federal prisoner got well enough to travel. He left out some naughty bits, since they were his own beeswax and a lady was present. But Marie still asked him whether he'd "gotten fresh with that cowgirl" before she was murdered.

Longarm washed down some grub with his coffee and growled, "Of course not. I was too busy playing slap-and-tickle with her Indians. Talking dirty about a dead lady who never wronged you is unbecoming to you, Miss Marie."

Marshal White quietly added, "I knew Miss Lorena Webber. Her brand was a running W and she only branded her own stock. There was some gossip about her staying out by Antelope Springs alone with a young and single foreman. But such gossip ceased when one of her married *vaqueros* drew in the Headquarters Saloon and swore he'd kill the next man who low-rated his *patrona,* who slept in the main house with two Mex maids behind locked doors."

John Clum said, "Lorena Webber's virtue or lack thereof is not the mystery here. You'd brought us up to those Indian guides leading you here, across the desert, with some plans on getting you together with their kinswoman, Clio Twill née Hendersen."

"*That* one's *loco en la cabeza!*" Marshal White declared. "I've had my boys watching out for her since she filed those baseless charges against her husband, Lester Twill. She's run off into the desert to live on lizard tails and cactus fruit with her Pima kith and kin!"

Longarm murmured, "Mebbe. But some say Lester Twill feels free to come and go as if they were happily married at the house she paid for on Sixth Street."

The town law frowned down at his coffee and growled, "He ain't supposed to go near the place. I'll have to have a talk with him the next time I see him."

Longarm said, "Good hunting. They told me at Fly's lodging house that he moved back to the Hendersen place. The Indian woman I talked to there said he wasn't there either, and he's quit the job he had at the assay office near John's *Epitaph*.''

John Clum brightened and declared, ''Maybe they've both been abducted by the same mysterious faction that just tried to kill or capture the two of you!''

Fred White muttered, ''Good riddance. That footloose prospector and his crazy fat squaw were no credit to the community.''

Longarm said, ''If you'd care for some educated guesses, I'd say the bunch who invited Miss Marie and me to supper were out for blood, and no matter where Lester Twill might be tonight, he told Cam Fly he wasn't worried about a woman who'd charged him with more than one felony turning up whilst he was in her town house.''

Marshal White nodded soberly and replied, ''That do look bad for young Lester, and if he ever turns up again he's going to need a good excuse for that. But you have to admit we can't do much to him on a suspicion alone. We can't hang a man without a corpus delicti, and as fat as she is, or was, there's an awesome amount of open desert around here to hide a corpus delicti pretty good!''

Longarm cut some more roast beef as he quietly pointed out that corpus delicti was lawyer talk for the *body of a crime,* and that a forged public record added up to a corpus delicti that might be way easier to find.

He said, ''It's getting late and I like to question each witness while earlier testimony is fresh in my mind. So I reckon I'd best start early and talk to that JP and the neighbors who signed those disputed wedding papers. What would you like for dessert, Miss Marie?''

She said she was torn between two types of cake, and confused by tuna pie. Longarm suggested she have both kinds of cake, and explained that when folks along the Mexican border mentioned ''tuna'' they were talking about cactus fruit instead of fish.

The three men exchanged looks when she demurely decided she'd try all three for dessert. Longarm had noticed, traveling with that opera company and Miss Sarah Bernhardt's Western tour, that singers seemed to like to keep their oral parts occupied. That was likely why folks who sang for their suppers tended to fatten up, drink themselves to death, or get arrested for public cocksucking.

As the still fairly slender and ever-so-proper soprano put away a heroic amount of coffee and dessert, Longarm and the thunderstruck men at the table wound up their discussion for the time being. White said he'd send word when their deputy coroner would want Longarm to drop by. Then the marshal and the newspaperman left Longarm alone with the sweet-toothed soprano, and their bill.

She didn't catch the laconic sarcasm when he politely asked her if she'd had enough. She dimpled across the table at him and confessed she couldn't swallow another bite. So he signaled the waiter for the tab. He was allowed six bits a day for grub as traveling expenses. She'd just put away that amount of grub at one sitting, and that reminded him what a spoiled brat she'd seemed earlier. So he was sincere and, being a woman, she could tell when she asked what came next and he calmly told her, "Nothing much, unless you'd care to sample some of that chocolate pudding on the menu. I'll carry you back to your hotel and they'll likely send you a summons if they want you to testify in front of the coroner's jury."

She stared wide-eyed as she demanded, "You expect me to spend the night on my own in this savage town with nobody defending me in case those awful men come after me?"

Longarm was lining up coins along the restaurant tab on the table as he replied, "You heard us agree those two who got away are likely long gone. It hardly pays to posse up after dark, and come morning, they could have too good a lead for anyone to bother."

She said, "But you said you thought somebody had *sent* them after us, the same as they sent somebody to blow you up in that other town, sent somebody else to murder that girl who'd talked to you there, and for all we know, kidnapped that unhappy couple who may or may not be joint owners of a silver mine! Can't you see they might send somebody *else* after *me*?''

Longarm left an extra quarter for their waiter, seeing he'd had to serve so many, as he dryly remarked, ''Anyone can see you're the most important gear in this mysterious cuckoo clock. If you're afraid to stay alone at the Grand Hotel, they might put you up for the night in the Tombstone Jail. In a private cell, I mean.''

She made a wry face and said, ''I'd rather stay with you, at your hotel, if you promise to be good.''

Longarm laughed and said, ''I ain't had too many complaints. But I can't promise anything silly, Miss Marie. I'm a man, and in spite of your sharp tongue, you're too tempting a woman to treat like a male drinking partner with no place to spend the night. They won't lock you up in the Tombstone Jail, you understand. I can't come up with a safer place for such a delicate flower.''

She started to cry. It didn't work on Longarm. He said, ''Let's go. We have to get us both holed up off the street *somewhere,* and we've agreed you don't want to spend the night with a natural man, the way natural men and women act natural.''

As he rose and held a hand out to her, she dabbed at her eyes and told him he was a brute.

He said, ''Have it your own way. If I wanted to play kid games, I'd find me a kid, and no offense, you're a woman grown with a mind of her own. So make up your mind where you want me to take you and I'll be proud to take you there.''

She timidly took his hand and rose to shyly ask, ''You will be gentle and you will use a condom, won't you?''

Chapter 15

Nobody was sure about the first name of the Dr. Condom who'd invented a device to immortalize his last name during the fornicating frenzy of the English Regency period. Mr. Charles Goodyear hadn't figured out how to vulcanize rubber that early, of course. So Dr. Condom's first efforts had been made from the handy-sized blind guts of sheep. Such condoms would still be marketed as "lambskins" a long time after stronger and cheaper ones made out of thin rubber hit the vast market for such devices between the California Gold Rush and the Civil War. The ones Longarm had packed in a saddlebag, with such an emergency in mind, were made of honey-colored rubber, and still cost a lot more than his cheroots.

But as he pawed around amid spare socks and shaving cream for the pillbox they came in, he reflected on the bright side. There was no way a man could use as many condoms as he smoked cheroots in a given twenty-four-hour period.

He was pawing because, at the soprano's request, he'd lit no lamps nor opened any window blinds as he led the way in and let her feel her own way to the bedstead, softly sobbing to herself.

He heard the rustle of silk as she sobbed and shucked

across the room in the dark. As he found the rubbers, he heard the bedsprings sigh, and set the pillbox aside on the bed table to sit down on the edge of the mattress and haul off his boots. He'd already hung his six-gun on the bedpost, after quietly removing the bullets. Women who came sobbing to a man's hotel room made a man uneasy.

He sneaked his double derringer in one boot and left that handy, near the head of the bedstead, before he unbuttoned any further.

Behind him, the gal who'd insisted on being there protested that she hoped he understood she didn't go to bed with every man she met. It wouldn't have been polite to tell her she'd be lucky to get many men to help her across the street. Had she been one lick less pretty, her abrasive flirting habits might have gotten her punched in the nose by this time.

As he undressed with mixed feelings about the whole deal, Longarm reflected on how women could wind up with sharper tongues than men, not because boys were born nicer than gals, but because boys were so much meaner than gals when somebody insulted them.

Little gals playing jacks could get away with spiteful comments about one another because an insulted female fought back with the same weapon, leading to lots of practice with rapier wit. But a boy who intimated that another boy shooting marbles with him needed a bath or had an ugly momma was likely to go home with a black eye. So boys learned young to watch what they said to others. It was *dangerous* for a man to carry on like the average nagging wife. That might have been why men with nagging wives seemed more confused than pissed.

Longarm let his pants fall anywhere they had a mind to, and swung his bare legs under the covers, where they touched bare unfamiliar flesh that flinched away. He slid his bare ass further down the bottom sheet as he reached for the pillbox of condoms under the trimmed bed lamp, saying, "It ain't too late to change your mind and if you do throw up, try to aim over the far side, will you?''

She softly replied, ''Please don't be so nasty, Custis. I'm trying to respond to you. It's not that I don't find you attractive. I guess it's because I keep picturing you with that horrid prima donna aboard that train. I could hear the two of you if I pressed my ear to the partition between our compartments, and the two of you seemed to be having so much fun as you made such vulgar sounds and said such nasty things!''

Longarm shrugged his bare shoulders and replied, ''Like I told you before, nobody was saying anything bad about you or anybody else.''

''What was that little piggy that went whee-whee-whee while she was gasping like that?'' demanded the curious understudy. ''Don't tell me you were playing piggies with her *toes*! It sounded as if she was having a climax to me!''

Longarm smiled fondly at the memory and confided, ''It sounded that way to the two of us as well. I'll show you, if you want.''

She stiffened as he moved closer and put a bare arm around her bare shoulders to draw her closer. Her naked flesh felt cool, and she bit her lower lip and hissed through her nostrils as he ran his free hand down her bare belly to where they both seemed to want it, since she didn't try to stop him as his questing fingers parted hair that might well be strawberry blond to search for the little Indian in the canoe.

When he found her clit, it was fully turgid and moist with desire in spite of her false modesty in such matters. He began to rock the little Indian in the canoe as she gasped, ''Oh, my God, that feels so much naughtier than when you do it to someone's toes!''

Then she reached for him, mocking, ''Whee, whee, wheeeee!'' until she had the matter in hand, gasped, and asked, ''What's the matter? Is it something I said?''

To which Longarm could only reply, ''Yep. I have yet to understand the prize you sharp-tongued ladies expect to win with those emasculating remarks. You've got me to be limp as a dishrag, and I hope you're really feeling triumphant.''

She began to stroke his disinterested organ-grinder as she insisted, ''I just said whee, whee, whee! I admitted your hand on my privates felt naughty. What more do you want? My complete humiliation?''

He said, ''I don't want nobody to feel humiliated. That's why I told you I thought you were good-looking instead of snotty when you came down the stairs at your hotel and told me to put out my smoke. This ain't going to work, Miss Marie. I know you're only nasty every third or fourth sentence. But it's like waiting for another round of shell fire when you're pinned down under enemy observation. At the risk of mixing metaphors, once a kitten scratches deep, I just don't feel like petting it much more. I'll see if I can make you come, seeing you're standing at attention down here. But don't worry about my old organ-grinder. Like I said, you've won. I just don't feel like fucking you, no offense.''

She wailed that they'd see about that as she rolled into position to suck his limp virile member as far in as it would go, trying to swallow the head as if it had been a raw oyster. And if the truth were to be known, that sent a tingle all through his crotch and down both legs as Longarm felt himself rising to the occasion.

It was tempting, but he didn't say anything as she felt the swelling in her mouth and got up on her hands and knees to keep taking it over the base of her tongue and a good way down her throat while she worked it up hard in all its glory.

Longarm chose his words with care, knowing how her defensive act had discouraged his own natural feelings. When he simply said, ''Let's finish right, honey,'' with nothing clever thrown in, she raised her head from his lap with one long lingering pull with pursed lips, then flopped limply on her own back and softly sighed, "I'd like that, Custis."

And she did, moving under him like a long-lost lover separated by, say, a war and missing him terribly until he could thrust his passion back where it had always belonged and forget all those superior airs.

He didn't say, he didn't have to, that the older opera star she'd been so jealous of had enjoyed it more with her makeup off, her hair down, and all her theatrical gestures cast aside to take it dog-style by the Pullman window in broad daylight while telegraph poles whipped by as her rosy rectum winked up at him in time with the clicking of railroad wheels. Remembering the rhythm inspired Long-arm to grind in and out of this younger opera singer at a pace she said she found inspirational, and when they came, remembering that more Junoesque brunette in broad day-light, and picturing this more Dianaesque blonde in the same position with sunlight shining in on them, he naturally had to roll her over and enter her dog-style in the dark.

She found that inspirational too, as she arched her spine to thrust her rump up to him, saying she'd never done it that way before and felt utterly depraved.

He didn't ask why so many women were willing to go dog-style while so few were willing to admit they'd ever done it with anyone else, or even that they just plain liked it, for no other reason than that it felt good.

Later, as they cuddled against the pillows piled against the head-rails, he told her a village-idiot joke as he groped on the bed table for a smoke and some matches.

Sensing what he was about, Marie pleaded, "Please don't strike a light. I'm not wearing a stitch!"

He gently but firmly replied, "I noticed. You've just had my cock down your throat and up your cunt. What are you afraid I might learn about you?"

This time she made him fell shitty as she cried quietly and he felt real tears on his bare shoulder. So he held her closer, kissed her, and said, "I won't strike a light. I'm sorry. That was a cruel thing to say, and I don't know why I said it!"

She quietly sobbed, "I do. My husband told me as he was packing. I *loved* him, Custis. I really loved him more than words could tell. Yet ever since I was a little girl, I've never been able to control my tongue, and I know how deeply it can cut. Why do I make such nasty remarks, Custis?"

He kissed her again and said, "I don't know for certain. I just now lashed out at you the same way, and speaking only for myself, I suspect I was paying you back. That's the trouble with tongue-lashing. One nasty crack deserves another and before you know it, someone's said something they can't take back."

"And someone's packing," she sighed, snuggling closer to confide, "I told him I was sorry. I told him I hadn't meant what I'd said about him never amounting to a thing as a tenor or a lover. I just now realized what he meant as he was going out the door. He told me I'd *won* as he slammed the door in my hysterical face. He meant I'd cut his balls off with my tongue, didn't he!"

Longarm softly said, "As far as you were concerned to *him,* you had. I suspect he soon found another gal who spoke more highly of both his voice and balls."

In a more mature voice than he'd ever heard from her before, she answered simply, "He did. I understand she's an Italian alto with huge hips and little knowledge of the English language. I understand they're very happy together."

Longarm didn't ask if the man who'd left her spoke Italian. He suspected he knew the answer.

After a long, comfortable snuggle, Marie told him she wouldn't mind if he struck that match now. So he did, and lit a cheroot for them both. But she demurely said she didn't like to smoke, and told him to light the bed lamp.

When he did, Marie declared, "Oh, you have a lovely body and I'm starting to feel the way Adam and Eve must have felt in the Garden before they'd sinned and felt any need for fig leaves."

He told her she was built pretty fine her ownself, and he meant it. For as nice as her trim body had felt in the dark, the sight of her strawberry nipples and strawberry-blond hair, all over, inspired a twitch of the love tool he'd just been using in her. Marie had sharp eyes as well as a sharp tongue. She said, "Tell me that joke about the village idiot again while you finish that smoke. I don't seem to get it, Custis."

Longarm blew a smoke ring to encircle one perky nipple as he told her, again, about the older boys taking pity on the village idiot and inviting him to tag along the next time they went to the village whorehouse. Once they got there, the madam wasn't sure they wanted to service an idiot. But one of the whores took pity on a poor fool with no brains and an immense virile member when he confessed he'd never had a woman. So she took him back to her crib, and for the next half hour they heard an immense slamming and banging with grunts and groans and screams and moans, until finally, the village idiot came out, grinning fit to bust.

Marie said, "That's where I get lost. I can understand why a kind-hearted bad girl might feel pity or even feel curious about a well-endowed youth who'd never had any. But what was it that the village idiot said when the other boys asked him how he'd liked it?"

Longarm replied, "He said it sure had pissing beat," and this time she laughed uncertainly and asked, "Is that all there is to fornication then, a slight improvement over urination?"

Longarm said, "Nope. A *great* improvement, and that may be why some folks get so mixed up about their love lives. On the one hand, poets write about moons, swoons, hugs, and kisses, whilst on the other hand, our elders are telling us not to get pee-pee or poo-poo on our hands or even look down yonder. So when lots of folks fall in love

127

and wind up in bed together, they don't know whether to come, piss, shit, or go blind, and the next thing you know, they're fighting over what ought to be pure pleasure."

Marie sighed, slid further down in the bed, and said, "You sound so much like my husband. But this time I'm going to *listen* when you tell me why I'm talking so silly. Leave the lamp lit and watch what I'm doing to you this time!"

So he did, and it made a man feel like one of those Turkish pashas while he enjoyed a relaxed smoke as he watched the part in a wild mop of strawberry-blond hair bob up and down while its owner took all a man had to give as far down her throat as she could take it.

But even as he was enjoying one of the best blow jobs he'd ever had, Longarm was wondering what in thunder he'd gotten himself into, aside from both ends of her. That shit about listening to him *this time* sounded as if she hadn't been paying attention when he'd said he'd be moving on, with a federal prisoner, as soon as he was able. He sure hoped she wasn't going to carry on like that other soprano had when he'd had to get off the Pullman at a northbound junction.

But he didn't want to hurt her before he had to hurt her, and as she caught him softly laughing, and paused in mid-suck to ask why, Longarm had to allow he was sorry he'd clean forgot to roll a rubber on down yonder.

To which Marie demurely replied, "That's all right. I know how to take care of myself and now that I know you better, I really do want you to enjoy it as much as *I* do, darling."

Chapter 16

Dawns didn't dawn so cold when a man woke up having breakfast in bed with a beautiful woman, and he seemed to be her breakfast. But later on, when they both got to eat breakfast downstairs after most of the town had been up and around a spell, Marie said she wanted to stay in the Cosmopolitan with him.

Longarm had long since decided that life was too short to use up much of it trying to argue with women. So he said she and her Saratoga trunks would be as safe at the Grand Hotel if he moved *there*. He added, "I could hire a dinky single on the sunny side, and nobody would have to know where I was really spending the siestas. You do have to sing at that saloon tonight, don't you?"

She demurely replied, "Just until one A.M.," and growled, "And I'm usually hungry when I get off work!"

So after they'd eaten he let her read the morning edition of Clum's *Tombstone Epitaph* by a lobby window while he went through the motions of leaving. He didn't want to really leave because everyone else, friend or foe, would expect to find him at the Cosmopolitan. He told the key clerk he'd be sending for his saddle later that morning if and when he hired a mount to do some riding. Then he escorted the strawberry blonde to her own hotel within walking distance, and sent her upstairs alone while he hired as cheap a garret room as they had on the premises. Then he went upstairs to tell her they were all set but he had to go back down and tend to some chores.

She said both their names were in the morning papers. So he sat on her bed and commenced to skim through both the *Epitaph* and its rival *Nugget* as the voracious opera singer commenced to unbutton his fly. He told her they didn't have time. But arguing with any woman down on her knees coud be a waste of time, and there was a lot to be said for whipping through the morning papers while you had a French lesson. It concentrated one's mind on the brass tacks because you just didn't care about the stock market or who might be running for office in the fall when you were fixing to come early in June, or Marie, as the gal was actually named.

John Clum had run his exclusive, as confusing as it might be to anyone who wasn't masterminding all the skullduggery. Longarm saw that both he and the lady with her head in his lap were being summoned before the deputy coroner's jury that afternoon. Clum had likely talked to others after they'd parted at the Can-Can Restaurant the night before. Longarm warned Marie they were likely to hear a knock on yonder door. But she just went on sucking with enthusiasm, and it somehow didn't seem to matter whether a process server knocked on the fool door or not.

The *Nugget* had less to say about the shootout in town, and missed any possible connection between Longarm's adventures up in Saguaro Wells and the attempt on his life in Tombstone. But being a paper that catered more to the country folk all around, the *Nugget* had scooped the *Epitaph* on the funeral arrangements for the late Lorena Webber. Her admiring obit said her murder was still under investigation by the sheriff in Tucson and a federal lawman from down the railroad line. They missed Longarm being the same one who'd shot it out with those unknown strangers the night before.

Miss Lorena's remains were being held above ground by the undertaker-cum-furniture merchant for her elder sister, a Widow Cleveland of San Antonio. Lots of newspaper editors who knew no better tended to spell San Antone its original Mexican way. Longarm was more surprised to learn Lorena Webber's only living kin was a widow woman. The *Nugget* said she'd been notified by wire when those Indians had brought her dead sister in, and that she'd be arriving by rail and then coach any time now for the funeral and probate of the will. They didn't say just who might have told them the dead gal had left her Running W spread and herd to her elder sister.

Marie had him so distracted, he almost missed the declaration Old Man Clanton had paid to have run on the same page. It tersely warned that the late Lorena Webber and her sister, the Widow Cleveland, had bounced on the knees of a younger N. H. Clanton in his Texas days, and that anyone trying to sell one head of Running W beef without a bill of sale was likely to wish he hadn't in the remaining minutes he had left.

Longarm read on the same page how those three unknown and unclaimed bodies from the warehouse fight would be held for as decent an interval as the climate of the Sonora permitted, and then buried in Potter's Field if nobody came forward for them. Longarm's respect for the *Tombstone Nugget* and its openly populist editorial slant went up a notch as he saw they'd resisted that irritating new fad of describing any Potter's Field in the west as "Boot Hill."

The one and only possible Boot Hill west of the Big Muddy had been, past tense, a prairie rise on the edge of Buffalo City, the market hunter's whiskey camp that had grown into Dodge City with the coming of the rails and a need to jerk engine water from the nearby Arkansas River. A few dead buffalo hunters and drifters had in fact been buried there informally, with their boots on. But soon after the township of Dodge City had been incorporated, they'd laid out their well-known Prairie Grove Cemetery and moved the dozen or so bodies buried inconveniently close out yonder downwind. So the one and only rise ever named Boot Hill had a schoolhouse and nary a dead man in his boots to brag on. The few transients nobody was willing to bury in any town, east or west, were planted at minimum public expense in the plots properly described as Potter's Fields because that was what the Good Book said they'd bought to bury dead paupers in, with the thirty pieces of silver Judas had left when he'd hanged his fool self.

Tossing the papers and caution to the winds, Longarm finished right in Marie on the rug, with both of them fully dressed. Then he said he was sorry, but he had to get back to work.

He left her to tidy herself, and went down to the lobby to bet the bell boy a dollar there was no way they could get his saddle and such from his room at the Cosmopolitan if he gave them a note and his room key. The bell boy asked if he could afford to lose two bucks, and Longarm pointed out he could hire a kid off the street for two *bits,* adding, "I put on a fresh shirt this morning because my older one was sweaty, not because I'm some English earl visiting the Great Southwest."

So they shook on a buck, and Longarm ambled over to Marshal White's office to see if anything the newspapers hadn't covered had turned up since they came out.

The deputy on desk duty handed him a note signed by the night man, Deputy Earp. It said nobody around town had seen hide nor hair of Lester Twill, but his wife, Miss Clio, seemed to be over at her town house on Sixth Street with half the Pima nation.

Longarm thanked the desk deputy and headed over to Sixth Street on foot, reflecting on that article in the *Epitaph* as he strode along in his shirtsleeves and vest with the morning sun staring him in the face. Having given John Clum a complete as well as exclusive account of his travails since getting off the train in Saguaro Wells, he'd naturally told Clum much of what Lorena Webber had told him, and the newspaperman had naturally made the most of that marital dispute and Clio Hendersen's silver lode in Chindi Canyon. Clum had done some homework on his own to add that they called the place Chindi or haunted because there were some deserted cliff dwellings over yonder, built way back when and then abandoned to the pack rats and rattlesnakes by a mysterious folk described as Hohokam by the Pima and Anasazi by Na-déné-speakers. The first term meant something like "People Who Got Used Up," while the other meant "Ancient Enemies." So the living Indians of both types refused to go near such ruins.

Considering some current Indian customs, Indians were more uncomfortable about the dead than Mexicans or even Anglo Americans. Mexicans, and Anglos to a lesser extent, visited the graves of dead kith and kin to leave fresh candlesticks, flowers, and such. Most Indians left their dead in peace and moved away. Some said the bites of rabid bats discouraged visits to deserted cliff dwellings as well.

Clum's description of the Hendersen Claim, as he called it, made Longarm suspect young John had seen a copy of the claim. He had it located further up the canyon than those ruins, with springwater, a fair amount of firewood in the form of high chaparral, and an assay of silver sulfide yielding eighteen to twenty dollars a ton as of now.

Longarm knew that while most silver lodes between the Rockies and the High Sierras tended to be silver chloride, there were outcrops of soot-black silver sulfide that were tougher to spot and easier to work.

A prospector had to know what he was doing if he hoped to spot a vein of silver sulfide because it looked like no more than a black streak across the country rock. Usually quartz but sometimes schist. But once you did figure out you were staring at silver ore instead of, say, an unprofitable coal seam, you only had to heat such ore over even an open fire to cook the sulfur out and leave molten silver to pour into ingot molds dug in the nearby dirt. So it was no wonder the heiress who'd been left such a claim and the mining man who'd assayed it for her felt like fighting over it whether they'd ever gotten married up or not.

Figuring he'd canvass that JP and the witnesses from next door once he'd talked to the reluctant bride, Longarm forged on to Sixth Street, ticked his hat politely to a soiled dove calling out to him, and told her he'd already had his morning blow job as he passed.

When he got to that spinach house with tomato trim, he found his two Pima pals, Little Eva and Topsy, squatting on the front steps as if they'd been waiting for him, with the hems of their cotton shifts scandalously high. As he strode to meet them he had to laugh, but then he sternly warned them, "You'd best cover your ring-dang-doos in public if you don't want to pay a twenty-dollar fine. It's not considered as public if you sit bare-ass in a window."

Little Eva said, "We just came from your hotel. They told us you had just left with a Saltu woman and we are both very cross. We were looking forward to fucking you in a Saltu bed before we brought you here!"

Topsy added, "There are Saltu beds inside. Maybe Porevo will let us use one with you, if we invite her to join us!"

That suggestion sounded even sillier when the door opened and that same fat housekeeper told him to stop flirting with those snips and come on in. When he did, Longarm found another fat woman waiting for him in a more nicely furnished front parlor than he'd imagined. The late Lorena Webber had told him her breed pal had been attending that finishing school when her father got hit by lightning.

It was easier to see why her Pima kin called her Porevo or She-Chief now. Aside from living much fancier than any pureblood, Miss Clio Hendersen was a head taller than most Pima men, thanks to her Scandinavian surname, most likely. She was also as fat as most desert dwellers could get after switching to a white man's far richer diet. Longarm sized her up as close to six feet tall, weighing close to 250 pounds. If Lester Twill had really thrown her down and raped her, he had to be one tough son of a bitch.

The facial features that went with all that lard were young and sort of pretty. Her big slanty eyes were set in her high-cheeked skull Indian-style. But they were that jade green you got by trying to mix eyes of cornflower blue with eyes of sepia brown. She wore her black but wavy hair pinned up, the way a white lady in such a fashionable summer frock of pongee silk might be expected to. She came over to give Longarm a gentle hug and a sisterly peck on the cheek as she told him Little Eva and Topsy had explained how he'd tried to help her old school chum Lorena. Her massive body smelled of regular bathing and jasmine perfume, likely French. A lady of fashion he'd slept with on a visit East had taught him that French perfumes always started out with a basic essence of jasmine, rose, or tuberose, with other smells tossed in to raise the ante. He almost hugged her back because she seemed more female at closer range.

She sat him on a leather chesterfield, and had that other fat lady fetch them some tea and crumpets as they talked. Nobody but a gal who'd been to a finishing school would have offered tea and crumpets in Tombstone to a man in shirtsleeves. But the crumpets were fair, cooked fancy as French crepes, but made with the local tortilla corn flour with enough lime to taste. Nobody born in North America, red, black, or white, knew how to make tea like an average Irishwoman.

Clio Hendersen said she was sorry she'd ever sent her poor school chum on such a fool's errand, and when Longarm asked why she thought he was a fool, she explained, "I don't mean you or Lorena were foolish. I meant I should have seen all along what Lester wanted. He wasn't after my body or my silver mine. He only wanted money!"

"You mean he's approached you for a payoff?" Longarm asked as he set the weak tea aside on a low-slung coffee table.

She said, "It was his lawyer, Edward Trevor, who sent word to me his client was thinking of moving on, seeing our marriage hadn't worked out. The lawyer said Lester was willing to forget and forgive if only I'd let him have a little traveling money."

Longarm asked bleakly, "How much did they shake you down for?"

She sighed and said, "Ten thousand dollars, with them offering a signed and notarized quit-claim renouncing me and all my property for all time."

"Without an annulment or divorce decree?" asked Longarm with a thoughtful frown.

She said, "We were never married. How could I get divorced?"

Longarm nodded soberly and said, "It sure does read like a fool's errand, Miss Clio. Until you consider the trouble somebody went to just to keep us from having this simple conversation."

"Do you suspect Lester of murder?" she asked saucer-eyed. Then she blushed and added, "He was awfully fresh with me, but he never really hurt me, and I simply can't picture him killing anybody!"

Longarm said he'd ask Lester Twill or his lawyer as soon as he caught up with either. Then he left to see if he could interview some others before it came time to rejoin Marie at the Grand Hotel for a siesta. As he headed away from the ever-rising sun, the Pima gals on the steps called a bawdy suggestion after him.

He had to laugh at that picture as well. It would likely kill any man who spent a siesta bare-ass with the blond Marie, the duskier Little Eva and Topsy, and the elephantine but sweet-smelling Porevo, or Clio Hendersen! But he couldn't help wondering if the four of them could be talked into such an interesting experiment.

136

Chapter 17

When Longarm went back to the Cosmopolitan Hotel to see if there were any messages for him, they told him two Pima squaws and a white man dressed for riding had been by earlier asking if he was in. He asked if the white man had been big and beefy. The clerk thought and allowed he had, now that Longarm mentioned it.

Longarm was almost sorry he'd mentioned it when that was all he could pin down. There were lots of big beefy riders. The cuss could have been there with a summons to that coroner's inquest, slated for later in the day. Longarm told the older man behind the counter to accept and hold any such writs as well as letters or telegrams. The hotel clerk looked disgusted, and said he'd been planning on wiping his ass with any papers addressed to a guest of the Cosmopolitan.

Longarm dug out that envelope John Clum had given him, and headed next to that JP's place where Lester Twill had married up with either Clio Hendersen, somebody else, or nobody at all.

When he got there, Justice of the Peace Will Dipple invited him in for coffee and cake in the kitchen while they talked about events he remembered tolerably.

As the old gray four-eyed JP's pretty Mexican *mujer*

served them both at the kitchen table, JP Dipple said he recalled the disputed wedding well because it hadn't been that long ago and because he'd wondered at the time why such a mismatched couple wanted to be married up.

Dipple explained, "The young prospector was a nice-looking gent if you don't mind weak chins. His bride-to-be was older, a big fat Indian squaw. When I told them they'd need approval of the BIA for such a union, they both swore she was a mostly white breed, living entirely white off the BIA rolls. So I said it was their funeral, and asked Mirt and George Montez from next door to act as witnesses. Do you want me to send Consuela here to fetch 'em?"

Longarm said that could wait, and asked, "You say the gal struck you as a full-blood, older than Lester Twill? How old would you guess *him* to be?"

The JP said, "Don't have to guess. His place and date of birth would be on the applications they filled out."

He rose to duck out as the *señorita* served Longarm and her hombre's empty place at the table. When he thanked her in Spanish, she blushed and ran into her pantry.

JP Dipple came back with a folded form, sat down by his own grub, and spread the single sheet across the unpainted pine to declare in a self-satisfied tone, "Here we go. Lester Twill, age twenty-seven, born in Nashville, Tennessee, and sprinkled Holy Roller. You ain't a Holy Roller, are you, Deputy Long?"

Longarm replied, "Nope. What can you tell me about the bride? That ain't their wedding certificate, is it?"

The JP said, "Of course not. Ain't you never been married? Nobody but me and the witnesses signed the screwing license I issued them. This is a copy of their *application* to get hitched. They have to fill 'em out and sign 'em in triplicate. I file one. Another goes to the county clerk in Tucson, and they get to keep one to show their lawyer if things don't work out."

Longarm reached out to slide the form closer as he

mused aloud, "Miss Clio keeps saying she never married Twill and . . . Thunderation! How come there's what looks like a Mexican cattle brand where it says she was supposed to sign?"

The JP shrugged and said, "I told you she was a squaw. That was her mark, so attested because she's an illiterate savage."

Longarm shook his head firmly and said, "No, she ain't. I just had tea and crumpets with her, and before that, Miss Lorena Webber was at a fancy finishing school with her. They don't let anyone sign up for a finishing school with a scribble that looks more like an antelope horn than anything else I can think of."

He thought back to his earlier talks with Lorena Webber, and added, "When her old school chum rode over to Tucson, the county clerk never mentioned any attested mark. They told her the records they had on file had been *signed* by her pal, period. Miss Lorena would have been mighty surprised to hear a gal she'd gone to school with didn't know how to read or write!"

The JP thought back and decided, "I'd have noticed if the copy for the county had been signed different than the one I was filing for myself. How would you go about switching a marked copy for any signed copy if you had one?"

Longarm said, "Easy, if you're a member of the courthouse gang with easier access to the county files than a stranger just asking. All you'd have to do would be to ask permission to copy some details for a client off their filed copy, then return your own *amended* copy to them as you were leaving. It's not that I don't admire this tempting layer cake, Your Honor. But I have to get over to Lawyer Trevor's office before he shuts down for La Siesta!"

So he almost ran as the sun rose higher, and just made it, catching the rat-faced Edward Trevor Esquire coming down the stairs from his second-story office.

Trevor held out a hand and allowed he was glad to see Longarm.

The overheated federal man said, "No, you ain't. I ran over to warn you not to cash any checks drawn on Clio Hendersen's bank account. I stand ready to back her claim in court that your client pulled some sort of a flimflam with another gal entirely the evening he swears he married Clio Hendersen!"

The rat-faced lawyer never batted an eye. He just sneered, "How do you propose to prove that, Deputy Long? Were you there? I fail to see you listed as a witness whether the wedding took place or not. As I explained to the fickle Miss Hendersen earlier, it's her word against his and no matter who might be telling the truth, we could hold up any development of that silver mine for months or even for years of litigation. I warned her that even if she wins in the end, it's going to cost her thousands in legal fees, and who's going to invest development money in a silver mine tied up in litigation?"

Longarm replied, "I just said it was a shakedown, with nothing to stop old Lester from coming back for more after the two of you split her first payoff."

He gently gathered a fistful of the lawyer's shirt as he quietly added, "I don't like to waste time telling a man what he already knows. But seeing you're an officer of the court, risking disbarment just as you've gotten in on the birth of a boomtown and a whole new county machine, I'll tell you why you don't want me backing Miss Clio in the courts of any county!"

"Unhand me, you uncouth rustic!" the lawyer tried.

Longarm shook him as one might a willful child and growled, "I'm trying to save your shingle for you. Your client showed up with what the JP describes as a fat pureblood, somewhat older than Lester Twill. I've just come from Clio Hendersen's. She looks more than half white, and I'd say she was around twenty-four on the date given

140

on those application blanks, which listed *him* as twenty-seven.''

Lawyer Trevor tried, ''My client said it was going on sundown, and you know how easy it is for an older man wearing specs in tricky light to misjudge such matters.''

Longarm said, ''Will Dipple don't wear specs, and there were other witnesses. But I'll concede that point if you'd like to tell me how come a woman who'd been to a fancy finishing school signed her form with a medicine sign like the illiterate pureblood she likely was.''

The lawyer said he hadn't seen such a mark on the copy his client had given him for safekeeping.

Longarm said, ''The copy filed in Tucson seems to have been signed in regular handwriting too. I reckon nobody could get at the original old JP Dipple filed in his own safe. The ringer your client brought before JP Dipple and his neighbors to marry up with may have been able to sign her name, but it wasn't Clio Hendersen, and there was an outside chance a neighborhood JP and notary public might have some other papers filed with the real Clio Hendersen's signature. I take it her real signature appears on any checks or bank drafts she's signed for you shakedown shits. But do your client and yourself a favor and don't try to cash any such paper. For like the Indian chief has said, I have spoken!''

He shoved the rat-faced lawyer back against the cedar siding of the balloon-frame office building, and let go of his shirt to walk away, shaking his head in disgust. There was an outside chance his warning might do some good. If the lawyer was in all the way with the clumsy and desperate extortionist, Longarm had only upped the ante by letting them know he was on to the old familiar game they'd been playing.

Marie Lamont said as much while they were talking about it dog-style during their siesta in her room at the Grand Hotel. She arched her supple spine to take him deeper from behind as she asked whether telling them right

141

out he was on to them might not encourage them to try again, more desperately than before.

As he held a hipbone in each cupped fist to thrust with his socks on the rug, Longarm calmly replied, "Nobody could try any harder than they did last night, and that sort of bothers me. Hiring five or more professionals when you're out to jump a claim would be one thing. A ten-thousand-dollar shakedown would be another. Lawyer Trevor is sure to demand at least a third, and a serious gunslick is going to ask at least five hundred for each try. I don't see how this game would be worth the candle to old Lester, do you?"

She lowered her cheek to the bedclothes and replied, "Could you move a little faster, dear? What if extorting that ten thousand from Clio Hendersen wasn't the original plan? What if you messed up their original plan simply by living through that ambush and so now all the survivors want is getaway money?"

He allowed that made some sense, and rolled her on her back to finish right with an elbow hooked under either of her wide-spread knees while she sobbed that she'd never ever let *him* get away now that she'd found him again.

He didn't argue. The few times he'd delicately mentioned the simple fact that his days in Tombstone were numbered, she'd gotten all teary-eyed and talked silly about coming to Denver with him and his prisoner as soon as Blacky Barnes could walk again.

They got washed and dressed to go out again around four, and he bought her some ice cream before they had to go over to the deputy coroner's hearing, held in a back room of the Oriental Saloon because the deputy coroner's house was too small and they hadn't built their new city hall and courthouse yet.

The hearing went smoothly enough. Miss Marie Lamont, a resident of Tombstone employed respectably, backed Longarm's story that he'd been invited for supper by an impostor pretending to be a mining investor, found he'd walked into a trap, and done what he had to do. Nobody there could come up with anything else he should have done. There was nobody to speak for the three dead strangers, and it looked as if Longarm had only shot two of them when you examined the bullets the sawbones conducting the autopsies had dug out.

They were hemming and hawing some about who those dead rascals had been working for when young Wyatt Earp, the head barkeep and part owner of the Oriental, came back to tell them the establishment was losing money all the while they kept the back room tied up. So the deputy coroner called a halt to the proceedings and the meeting broke up.

Longarm took Marie on over to the Crystal Palace, seeing it was almost time for her to entertain there with her pretty face and high-toned singing. They ate supper together across the way, and he watched her first performance from the Crystal Palace bar. But then it was time to get back to his own chores. So he legged it over to the Cosmopolitan Hotel to ask if there were any new messages or whether that mysterious rider had come looking for him again.

The clerk handed him a telegram and told him the pale gray-haired lady in a gray travel duster, seated across the lobby amid a pile of baggage, had been asking for him.

First things coming first, Longarm tore open the telegram to find it was from his home office, sent day-letter rates, or in odd dots and dashes when the wires weren't busy with regular traffic. Longarm saw why as soon as he read it. Billy Vail wanted to relieve his mind by offering to send someone else to pick up Blacky Barnes if he was on to anything really hot in Tombstone.

Reflecting that everything was hot in Tombstone at that time of the year, Longarm ambled over to the gray lady, deciding she was really a trail-dusted ash-blond of around thirty as he got close enough to doff his Stetson and introduce himself.

She extended a gloved hand, saying, "I'm Melony Cleveland. I understand you were friends with my poor little sister, Lorena Webber?"

Longarm shook with her, saying, "I knew her up in Saguaro Wells and I'm pure sorry about what happened to her, Miss Melony. She told she had a married sister back in Texas. I just learned this morning you were coming out our way as a widow woman. So I'm sorry about that as well."

She sighed and said, "So am I. Tom and I had a good marriage. The reason I came here this evening when I heard you were staying here is that I have nobody else here in Tombstone to turn to!"

He put his hat back on as he replied, "Do tell? I thought your kid sister left you a going cattle spread, complete with a staff of hired help."

She nodded and said, "They're expecting me to arrive tomorrow. I wired them to meet my stagecoach here in Tombstone then. I made much better connections along the way from San Antone than they'd led me to expect and . . ."

"They've been making up for lost time laying rails in Texas," he explained now that he understood her problem. "It's about a three-hour round trip out yonder and back if I hire a buckboard right away. So you just sit tight here with your baggage and I'll run over to the Dexter Livery and hire one, hear?"

She said, "You have to let me pay the livery fee, and I just hate to impose on anyone like this. But I don't know anyone else and . . ."

He cut her off with; "You don't need to know nobody else. Your kid sister would want me to carry you home, and to tell the truth, I wanted a look at your Running W in any case."

144

Chapter 18

The Running W was eight or ten miles to the northeast of Tombstone, and she'd ridden a good part of the afternoon from the northeast. But the long hairpin across the desert didn't seem to vex Melony Cleveland née Webber all that much. She said the Sonora was a prettier desert than they had around San Antone, with its mesquite and prickle-pear stretched out across flatter country.

As they drove along in the moonlight with her steamer trunk and two Saratogas in the buckboard bed behind them, they had plenty of time to get to know one another better. Like other Victorians, they were used to ignoring body functions Queen Victoria denied in a world running on steam and horsepower with precious little indoor plumbing. So neither mentioned the farts and shit falling out of the mules in front of them, or the midway stop she asked for so she could see if there were any flowers to pick on the far side of some cholla. Longarm snuck a piss on the far side of the team while they were at it.

By this time, he'd already learned that she'd come to stay and meant to run the spread her kid sister was leaving her. Her late husband had been another owner's foreman back in Texas, and when her sister, Lorena, had invited him to ramrod the Running W, he'd been too proud to work for kin. His widow remembered him fondly, but with just a tinge of bitterness when she considered how little they'd had in the bank when her Tom and his pony were run over by a stampede. She said it seemed ironic that a younger pal of her Tom had wound up in charge of the Running W for her sister, and so now *he'd* be working for *her*.

Longarm said he'd heard there was an Anglo ramrod along with a handful of Mexican help. She said she'd never been as handy with Spanish as Lorena, but trusted a boy she knew from home not to insult her in Spanish with strange Mexicans.

As they drove along, walking the mules up the rises and trotting them down, she explained how Bobby MacBean, the boy next door as the three of them had been growing up outside of San Antone, had blossomed into a top hand admired for his Spanish and other social skills by the *señoritas* at the fiestas out front of the Alamo.

Longarm chose his words before he said, "I heard talk in town about him being a sort of dashing young gent working well out of town for a single woman. You'd have known whether there was anything to such gossip, wouldn't you, Miss Melony?"

She laughed incredulously and replied, "Lorena and Bobby MacBean? He was like a big brother to her back home. There was nothing between them like that. He used to call her Skippyloo, and she'd have never sent for him if she'd thought he felt any different. *I* was the one he took to Sunday-Meetings-on-the-Green now and again. We were closer in age and he couldn't take any of the Mexican girls he knew to a Methodist picnic, see?"

Longarm said, "I'm starting to. Have you considered it might be a tad more awkward for yourself out yonder with a boy you used to picnic with taking orders from you?"

She sighed and said, "It will be good to be with at least one old friend from home. Bobby and my Tom rode together, and come Sunday, the two of us will be riding this very trail the other way to lay poor Lorena to rest. Bobby arranged all that with the Methodists in Tombstone before he wired me about her death. Why are we stopping?''

Longarm reined the team to a total halt in the shadows of some trailside organ-pipe cactus as he calmly reached for the Winchester '73 he'd brought along and quietly said, ''Somebody riding funny along our backtrail. Sounded like two ponies.''

She cocked her ash-blond head to listen tight before she decided she didn't hear anything.

Longarm murmured, ''Neither do I. That's what I mean by funny riding. It's a free country. This is a public right-of-way. So why would anyone pace a buckboard a quarter mile ahead so shyly? They've been trotting uphill as we've been trotting down, walking on the downslope as we've been walking up, and as you can hear for your ownself, they reined in when I reined in just now.''

''Who do you think they could be?'' she gasped.

To which he replied, ''They could be anybody. That's why I'm fixing to help you down and walk you around to the far side of this clump of organ-pipe whilst Mr. Winchester and me find out who they could be. If I lose, start running. We ain't too far from town for you to make it back on foot before the sun comes out to fry you.''

She sobbed, ''Oh, Dear Lord! Why would they want to murder my poor sister and then come after me?''

Longarm dropped off the buckboard on his side to circle the tailgate silently. But as he helped her down from the sprung seat, he told her, ''They might be after *me*, ma'am. You wouldn't have heard about it aboard your train from Texas, but I shot it out with some gunslicks about this time last night. I'll know the two who got away if ever I see them again.''

As he led her around to the far side of the clump of tall skinny cactus, her high-buttons crunching through the caliche louder than his bigger low-heeled boots, she asked if they'd been the same men who'd killed her sister.

He said, ''One of them might have been, ma'am. The

Pima riding with her when she was shot from ambush made it one rider on one shod pony. Before you ask me why, I'm still working on that. Stay here and I'll ask if I can get the drop on 'em.''

But as he circled back to the buckboard and its hired team on the trail, he heard what sounded like distant singing coming closer. He knew the old trail song, having ridden many a long dusty trail before he'd ridden for Marshal Billy Vail. Somebody was bellowing out of tune:

> Come and tie my pecker to a tree, to a
> tree.
> Come and tie my pecker to a tree!

Longarm fired at the stars and levered another round in the chamber as he called out, ''Hold off on the next verse, boys. There are ladies present.''

The singing stopped, but the riders didn't. As they bore down on him, one called, ''Who's that and what ladies are we talking about?''

Longarm called back, ''I'd be U.S. Deputy Marshal Custis Long on the way to the Running W with its new owner, the Widow Cleveland, if it's all the same with you.''

He could see the four of them riding abreast in the moonlight now. Three seemed Anglo cowhands. One was wearing a charro outfit and a Mexican sombrero. As they got within easier talking distance, one said, ''Johnny Ringo told us you was in town. I'm Ike Clanton. The handsome brute to my left would be Bill Graham. Yonder to my right is my baby brother, Finn, and we call this greaser Maldito because he won't tell us his real name.''

Longarm laughed and said, ''Curly Bill and me go back a ways. How come you ain't in jail this evening, Bill?''

The man occasionally called Bill Graham or Brocius, depending, laughed and replied in an easy tone, ''Evening, Longarm. Like I told you the last time, you ain't got nothing federal on this child. How come you have that Winchester in your hands, Uncle Sam?"

Longarm said, "Before I heard your dirty singing, I heard someone else trailing us from town. Sounded like two of 'em, riding bashful. You boys must have scared them off."

Ike Clanton turned to Maldito to say, *"Bueno, vuelve y mira."*

As the *vaquero* turned back to scout the edges of the trail, Longarm called Melony forth and introduced her to the members of the Clanton Gang. To their credit, all three removed their hats, and Ike Clanton said, "We were right sorry to hear about your sister, Miss Melony. Our dad says he knows your kin back in Texas, and if there's anything any of us can do for you, Miss Melony, you'll never have to ask it twice."

Young Finn Clanton shyly said, "I met up with your kid sister as we was both hunting strays out in the cactus. She was purdy. You got my word as a man that the ones who shot her in the head will die shot in the guts if ever we find out who they were."

Longarm said, "They might not be that far, and Miss Melony might feel safer if you boys cared to ride with us on out to her place."

Ike Clanton said they'd be honored. When Melony said she hoped it wasn't too far out of their way, Ike Clanton snorted, "You let us keep track of the few extra miles, Miss Melony. We'd rather *walk* that far than answer to our daddy for deserting one of the Webber gals on the trail with others spooking her!"

So Longarm got the two of them back aboard the hired buckboard and they were all on their way. Maldito caught up with them to report he'd cut the sign of two ponies turning off into the caliche to circle back toward Tombstone. He added, "They would make it to the Oriental and have that *alcahuete* young Earp, lying for them by the time we could catch up, I think."

Melony asked if *alcahuete* meant something like alcoholic in Spanish, and Longarm had to laugh too before he soberly assured her it meant something. Maldito had only switched to Spanish because he hadn't wanted to describe the night manager of the Oriental as a pimp in front of a proper lady.

Longarm quietly told Ike Clanton he seemed a mite harsh on the kid brother of a town deputy. The reputed stock thief switched to Spanish to ask what else you'd call a man who served women without escorts at the bar.

He went on to complain that Union vet Virgil Earp accused him and his Confederate kin every time some Mexican kid swiped an apple off a fruit stand.

Longarm asked if it wasn't true the Clantons had sold a few head of beef to the BIA bearing unusual brands. Curly Bill cut in to explain without a trace of shame, "We only run the brands of purely Mexican cows. It served the greasers right for Goliad and the Alamo. But we never raid Anglo herds, Longarm. That would be dishonest!"

Ike Clanton went on to insist he and his kith and kin had been mistreated by that Damnyankee dude John Clum in his lying rag, the *Tombstone Epitaph*.

Longarm didn't argue. He knew that there were three sides to every story: the one side, the other side, and the truth. Educated men who longed for law and order were inclined to take a jaundiced view of any rowdy rustics, and there was no denying the Clantons and their pals were rowdy and rustic. On the other hand, the Clantons had too many admirers, including everyone writing for the *Tombstone Nugget*, to be all bad. So Longarm was willing to wait and see.

Meanwhile, the company of the rowdy Clantons made Longarm feel a whole lot safer along the moonlit trail across the desert as it wound up into the higher chaparral of the Dragoon foothills. Melony laughed and clapped her hands when Ike Clanton pointed into the darkness with his quirt at some shady shifting blurs to call out in a cheerful tone, "Them cows over yonder under that smoke tree belong to you, Miss Melony. Fifty acres of the Sonora can graze one cow."

Longarm didn't ask Ike Clanton how he read brands after dark. The Clantons had declared in print that the Running W herd was under their protection. It was comforting to see they'd meant what they'd paid to have published. Both the publishers and the Bureau of Indian Affairs said the Clantons had never been *caught* running brands registered north of the border. They likely felt they didn't have to. A side of beef was a side of beef to a hungry Indian, and they sure raised fine Andalusian longhorns just to the south. It was a toss-up whether the Earp brothers or outraged Mexicans were liable to kill Ike or Old Man Clanton first. But Melony Cleveland née Webber could have had less neighborly neighbors over in the foothills of the Dragoons.

They finally drove into the sprawling moonlit 'dobe sprawl of the Running W, where Bobby MacBean and a whole tribe of laughing Mexican men, women, and children came out in the dooryard to greet their new *patrona*.

Longarm and the Clanton Gang got to follow Melony and her ramrod into the big house for a tequila rest-up before she had the bath and good night's sleep she likely needed after so many hours by rail and stage. Bobby MacBean, or Bob as he asked the other menfolk to call him, said she'd caught them completely by surprise, arriving so early. He said, "I wired you the morning those Indians carried Miss Lorena in off the range to Tombstone, Miss Melony. But you sure must know how to settle up and pack your bags before the next train comes through!"

Indoors, by lamplight, Bob MacBean was in fact a slim-waisted and broad-shouldered young gent with ginger hair and mustache who might have seemed a pretty boy if he hadn't looked so tanned and muscled up. Like the Clantons, he dressed for riding the thorny Sonora in shotgun chaps, a loose Basque shirt such as Navajo wore, and despite being on his home spread, a brace of Navy Colt conversions, carried cross-draw on either horseman's hip.

Longarm noticed Melony had greeted him like a kissing cousin indeed. She was doubtless comforted, after all those many miles among strangers, to meet up with the boy next door who'd courted her some before she'd married a more serious swain. Longarm knew enough about the consoling of widow women to feel a tad jealous of the good-looking squirt, now that he saw Melony out of that shapeless travel duster and in a summer print bodice and Dolly Varden dress she filled out so nicely. Time's cruel teeth had been kind to the older of the Webber girls. She was built like a brick shithouse.

She was as nice as her kid sister had been too. She invited all of them to bunk the rest of the night at the Running W if they had a mind to. Ike Clanton and his bunch allowed they'd get on home, now that they could tell their old man they'd seen the lady safely to her own dooryard. Longarm wasn't certain, but he suspected he'd detected a look of relief in Bob MacBean's blue eyes when Longarm allowed *he* had to be back in Tombstone by midnight lest his hired buckboard turn into a pumpkin.

Driving back alone with his locked and loaded Winchester across his knees, Longarm felt mighty lonely in the moonlight.

This was partly because those riders who'd been tailing him the other way might have been smart enough to assume he'd be coming back to town to meet Marie after work, and partly because he was driving back to town to meet Marie after work.

He was sort of looking forward to another roll in the feathers with the strawberry-blond shrew he'd tamed. But when all was said and done, what could you do with a tamed shrew that you couldn't do as well or better with a Junoesque ash-blond widow woman who seemed to treat all men considerately?

Chapter 19

Longarm wasn't really jealous of Bob MacBean until he was having breakfast with Marie after a night of unusual passion, even for her. She waited until they were having coffee after their eggs over chili before she said she had to catch the stage to Tucson and asked if he cared to ride with her as far as Frisco.

When he asked why she had to go all the way to Frisco, she explained that the *San Francisco Examiner* had run the story of that shootout the night before last and that a Frisco booking agent had wired her a job offer she just couldn't refuse.

Longarm smiled like a good sport and reached across the table to pat her wrist, saying, "That just goes to show that it pays to advertise, and I'm proud of you, honey. It ain't often I turn in with an understudy and wake up with a famous opera singer."

She fluttered her lashes and repeated her offer to screw him all the way to Frisco Bay. He resisted the temptation to suggest she save some for that booking agent. It sure beat all how pissed off a man could feel when a woman he'd been worried he was stuck with said she was leaving him. Like most lawmen, Longarm could tell many a tale of outraged husbands who'd killed the wives they'd been cheating on.

He told her he had to make sure Clio Hendersen put a stop on any check she'd written for the blackmailing Lester Twill. When the high-strung soprano asked what Clio Hendersen looked like, he truthfully replied, "She ain't changed much since the last time you asked. I told you she'd run off past pleasantly plump into just plain fat. Pima ain't as used to tea and crumpets as the rest of us."

He felt no call to tell her Little Eva and Topsy hadn't been eating *saltuduka* or white man's grub long enough for it to show. He toted her baggage to the stage depot for her, and bought her some candied ginger to nibble aboard the coach if she started to get seasick. For some reason she was crying as he helped her aboard and wished her luck.

The one bank in town, Safford, Hudson & Company, didn't open until nine. But it was closer than Clio Hendersen's place. So Longarm bought a fresh copy of the *Epitaph* to read as he waited, sitting on the steps out front in his shirtsleeves while the morning heated up.

He saw they were holding Lorena Webber's funeral at First Methodist on Sunday, that morning being Friday. John Clum predicted a big turnout for such a popular cattle-woman. Longarm prefered not to dwell on the closed-casket service they'd surely have. He'd been to a war one time, and it was all too easy to picture someone who'd been shot in the head with a .50-caliber slug that many mornings back. They'd no doubt embalmed her and stored her some-where cooler than the steps of that fool bank. But those Indians had had to haul her a long way just plain dead, and she'd been a pretty little thing too.

Two of the three corpses he and his derringer had do-nated to the local Potter's Field had been planted *there*, wrapped in cottin ticking and unpreserved, no doubt. But the *Epitaph* said they were holding one corpse a traveling salesman had identified as the remains of the late Mormon Jim Reynolds, a hardcase from Utah Territory. Marshal

White had told John Clum that Reynolds wasn't really a member in good standing of any particular church. But it paid to advertise, and so Mormon Jim had been the professional name of a paid assassin. The wanted papers out on the killer from Utah Territory said his usual asking price was five hundred dollars, but that he could be talked down to as low as fifty when business was slow. John Clum was inclined to write sort of sardonically. So you had to take his local color with a grain of salt. But he usually had his names and basic facts they way he'd heard them.

His big story, written tongue-in-cheek to rival Mark Twain, was the saga of the dashing desert prospector and his reluctant halfbreed bride. The *Epitaph* didn't seem to connect that shootout in the half-built warehouse with Clio Hendersen and her silver mine or the murder of Lorena Webber. Longarm was sure John Clum suspected they were tied in together. But the domestic difficulties of the joint claim owners read funnier with nobody getting hurt. Longarm had to smile as he read the amusing way the paper repeated the charges and counter-charges, with her calling him a fortune hunter out to jump her claim and him implying he'd expected way more passion from a well-fed Pima.

Then the bank was open, and Longarm went in to toss the paper in the waste barrel and ask to see their manager as he flashed his federal badge.

But all he found out was that Clio Hendersen didn't have an account with Safford, Hudson & Company. They suggested she might have a bank account in Tucson or back in Yuma if she'd been paying her Tombstone bills by check. So he thanked them and said he'd ask her.

But when he got to Clio Hendersen's place on Sixth Street, that fat housekeeper said her boss lady had gone out for the day. She didn't know where. Longarm was about to leave when the far skinnier and prettier Topsy came out from the back to calmly ask him if he'd like to fuck her before it got too hot that morning.

Trying not to meet the eye of the older Pima woman,

Longarm allowed it was already warming up, and asked Topsy if she knew where the gal she called Porevo had run off to.

Topsy said Clio and the other young gal they called Little Eva were on their way to Chindi Canyon with some mining men. Topsy explained she had been there more than once, and didn't like the way the spirits of the cliff-dwelling Hohokam had been staring down at her from the black doors and windows of their ruins in the sky.

Longarm asked how come Clio and the other young gal were riding up Chindi Canyon with other white men. Topsy shrugged inside her thin shift and replied, "They said something about lending her the money to put up buildings and sink deeper holes where her father had found black rocks." Topsy added, "I think black is a medicine color of the Hohokam. Porevo says her father died not long after he brought that black rock down from those hills. They are bad hills. Our nation used to fight the Apache in those hills, long before you Saltu Taibo came out here to fight them. There may be Apache spirits in Chindi Canyon too. It is not a safe place to play *nanipka* with the spirits of the long-dead Hohokam. Porevo should let them keep the black rocks her father found there."

Longarm said, "We might be able to get there ahead of Miss Clio and her business associates if you'd lead the way around and beyond them, seeing you know the way. So how about it, Topsy?"

The sultry Pima gal asked, "Why do you want to play *nanipka* with Porevo and those other Saltu Taibo?"

On a second hearing Longarm recalled that Ho kids playing the game they called *nanipka* were playing hide-and-seek the same as white kids. He said, "I'll tell you along the way. Where are your own riding mules right now?"

She said they were at the Dexter Corral, and asked if he'd fuck her when their game of *nanipka* was over. So he promised, sure Billy Vail would approve fornication with an Indian in the line of duty, and the two of them scampered over to the Grand Hotel along the way to pick up his saddle and Winchester, ignoring some mighty odd looks they got.

Longarm didn't have to hire his own saddle mule from the livery, seeing Topsy could produce four for the two of them. As they rode out to the east at a trot, Topsy said the others had close to an hour's lead on them if you counted from Clio leaving the house. But Topsy thought, and Longarm agreed, she'd likely screwed around in town getting all those businessmen set to hit the trail across the desert.

The Pima girl set a course through the cactus a tad more to the southeast than Longarm had expected. When he said this during a trail break, Topsy called him a *kokopelli,* and added that he'd *asked* her if they couldn't circle wide of those other riders.

They changed mules and rode on. Longarm had just recalled how a *kokopelli* was a painted clown with bells on at Pima harvest rites when he spotted the dust of a larger party off to the north and told her she was right. He didn't ask whether those other riders would be able to make out Longarm and Topsy's dust. He didn't want to be called a clown again. He knew they already had, but with any luck, might dismiss any riders off to their south as cowhands heading somewhere else. Long before he and Topsy were forging up an alluvial fan toward the wide gap in the chaparral-covered foothills to the east, he'd lost sight of that other bunch they'd left far behind.

As they rode further, the hillsides to either side gave way to the steeper walls of a true canyon, rising ever closer and steeper as they came upon a soggy patch of sand, and then an ever-deepening braided stream running down the center of the stupendous canyon it must have taken millions of years to excavate, allowing for more water after a heavy rain. Tall sedge, crackwillow, and alder lined the banks of the canyon's creek as they rode further in. As they were rounding a bend, Topsy called back, "Watch out for Pia-muhmpitz! If he is anywhere it must be around here!"

Longarm had heard the name of the top Ho ogre before. Piamuhmpitz seemed to combine the worse features of a man-eating giant and a big old cannibal owl. Indians seemed to see no contradiction in spirits that shifted in the telling from man to beast. When an Indian said Coyote or Raven did so-and-so, they likely pictured a critter something like you saw on the wall of ancient Egyptian tombs.

As Longarm and Topsy passed under the cliff dwellings high above, he saw why she found that stretch of canyon spooky. There was something about the dozen or more staggered square structures stuck like wasps' nests along a narrow ledge under an overhang that spooked *him*, and Longarm didn't believe in cannibal owls.

He'd climbed up to other cliff dwellings from time to time, but not unlike most Indians, he tended to leave them be. Sometimes you found dried-up dead folk in the back rooms, and you always found bat shit and pack-rat droppings. No Indians, but some whites, searched for pottery and such in such ruins. But the pottery was almost always deliberately broken by the ancient cliff dwellers who'd left it there with their dead, and even when it wasn't, Longarm figured it didn't belong to him and hadn't been meant for him.

As they rode under the last cluster of cliff dwellings, Longarm spotted some shards of freshly broken red pottery along the base of the cliff. He grimaced in disgust. Somebody prospecting the canyon in more recent times had poked about up yonder. He hoped they'd been bitten on the ass by bats.

Topsy led him further up where the canyon went blind in a sort of steep-walled arena rising in a semi-circle around a bubbling spring.

As they dismounted, Longarm saw that most of the alder and willow one might expect in such a natural Eden had been cleared for firewood. A considerable pile of wood-ash back from the water told him where most of it had been burnt. Some tent pegs were still in the ground to show where past and more recent prospectors had camped by the source of the canyon creek. As they tethered the four mules to stumps, Longarm asked Topsy if she knew where the outcrop of silver sulfide might be.

She said, "No. I was not here when Porevo's father found the black rock, or when that man who raped her broke off some more to have it tested in Tombstone at the place he worked. You promised to fuck me if I brought you here. I have brought you here and I like the way you fuck. So what are we waiting for?"

Longarm reached out to her, but said, "It ain't that I've forgotten your own sweet little ring-dang-doo, Skookum-chuk. But I just hate to get caught with my pants down literally, and those others will be along any minute now!"

Topsy stepped closer to flatten her small firm form against him as she protested, "They won't be here for an hour as your own people measure the day. Where did you learn to call a girl Skookumchuk? I think you must have fucked Ho Hada girls before!"

Longarm chuckled, kissed her, and confessed, "When you're right you're right. Where did you *think* I learned? But no offense, I don't want to take off this gun rig and strip to my birthday suit under the noonday sky with Lord knows how many others about to ride in on us!"

She insisted, "You said you wanted to beat them here. So we beat them here by riding through the time when Tanapah stands highest in the sky. They will have stopped to seek shade out on the open desert. If they start out again early, they will not be here for a long time. So why don't we take off our clothes, jump in that cool water, and fuck like frogs?"

He laughed and said, "Lord knows that sounds romantic. But with my luck they've pushed on for the shade of his canyon instead of holing up under cholla or a smoke tree."

She said he hated her because she was Ho Hada, and started to cry.

Longarm kissed her again and said, "I wish you

wouldn't do that. I'll tell you what. Why don't we clamber up to those cliff dwellings where nobody can surprise us and have a little slap-and-tickle in private? Should we hear anybody riding in, we'd have time to put our clothes or, hell, finish coming, before anyone worried about our mules comes looking for us.''

Topsy gasped. ''You expect me to fuck you in a haunted house on the side of a cliff? What kind of a girl do you think I am?''

He told her. So she laughed and confessed the notion of feeling a mite scared while she was screwing sounded sort of interesting. She added, ''When I brag about this day while baking *piki* with the other girls, I can say I wondered how many Hohokam spirits were watching as I fucked the famous Saltu ka Saltu!''

So Longarm made sure the mules could get at the water and browse the little fresh sedge by the spring, before he took Topsy's hand some more and led the way up a narrow path and then some handholds the long-gone Hohokam had cut from the rock to get down to the water.

Once they were up on the main ledge, the string-bean settlement of roofless square dwellings with just a few slit windows seemed bigger, with more safe room to explore. Still leading Topsy with his left hand, Longarm worked in toward the native rock as he told her there had to be some nice shady place to undress in.

Then, just as he was leading her around a corner of tan freestone, something that sounded like an angry hornet whizzed past his ear and almost parted Topsy's hair as the sound of a rifle shot caught up with it.

''*Piamuhmpitz!*'' Topsy wailed, trying to break free as Longarm went for his six-gun with his free hand.

Then they were both crouched on the safer side of that corner as Longarm hissed, ''Be still and keep your head down! Whoever that might be with that rifle up ahead, I doubt like hell it's a cannibal owl!''

Chapter 20

Longarm left Topsy holed up with his derringer in a blind slot as he tried to follow his hat on a gun barrel around that same corner.

Somebody shot his Stetson off with a .44-40. There had to be some better way. He glanced up at the ancient sun-silvered cedar vigas poking out of the freestone wall like a row of cigars. Vigas were an American Indian invention the Spanish colonists had quickly seen the advantage of. The vigas you saw sticking out of Pueblo or Mexican 'dobes weren't there for decoration. They were the ends of the log rafters holding the flat earthen roofs up. So Longarm holstered his six-gun and grabbed for a viga eight feet up as he jumped in his stovepipe boots. He grabbed the dry splintery cedar, and hauled the rest of him up to fork one leg over the edge of the wall and roll cautiously on up and over.

The caution was called for because the tamped earth over lighter brushwood was long gone. The eight vigas that had once held them now spanned the empty chamber below like sagging telegraph poles. He dropped down to the clay floor and eased over to a narrow slot that faced in the direction of those rifle shots. He couldn't see all of the rifleman. Just the barrel of his rifle peeking around the corner of another structure across a ten-or-twelve-foot gap. Longarm braced his six-gun and fired, knocking the rifle barrel out of sight as it stung the other's hands like hell if he or she had managed to hang on to it.

When he heard the scuffle of retreating leather, Longarm put his six-gun away again to haul himself over that far wall and dash across to the one he'd just chased somebody away from, drawing again as he dashed.

There was another loophole in the wall he flattened against to let his heart catch up with him. He called out, "We'd best talk it over, friend. I'd be U.S. Deputy Marshal Custis Long and I have you boxed. I thank you for not shooting down at us as we rode in just now. But as you surely know, we're betwixt you and the only way to the springwater down below. Who are you and what are you doing up here?"

There was no answer. But Longarm heard more motion, even further away. So he risked a peek through the closer loophole.

On the far side, he saw how somebody had been camping in that roofless shell. The rock overhang above kept the interiors of all the old structures dry in all but the most serious summer thunderstorms.

Longarm tallied up the water bags, firewood, canned goods, and one sleeping bag as he muttered aloud, "One crazy hermit or a guard left to watch the layout down yonder. In either case, somebody brung you and then led the mount you rode somewhere else. The two of you were counting on the most ferocious Bronco Apache being too spooked by the Chindis to pester you up here!"

He eased around the no-longer-covered corner, calling out, "Give it up and let's talk! I ain't out to arrest nobody just for jacking off up here. What's this all about?"

A distant male voice sobbed, "This is private property! Go away or I'll have to kill you!"

Longarm called back, "I can't go away. I'm on duty. You had your chance to kill me and you never did. So I'm counting that in your favor and here I come. If you kill me now, I'll never speak to you again!''

He thoughtfully reloaded before he forged on, having to consider the repeating rifle in the other man's hands. He tried not to make a sound as he pussyfooted around two and then three more corners. But the mysterious other either heard or suspected his intent, because Longarm heard him shout, ''Don't come any closer! I mean it!'' followed by a shrill womanly scream that seemed to fade off in the distance as the screamer moved off mighty suddenly.

Longarm edged over to the drop-off through a gap between two other empty shells, and sure enough, he could make out the sprawled figure of an unfortunate in faded denim spread-eagled on the rocky floor of the canyon between his hat and rifle.

Longarm whistled and said, ''I'll bet that smarted!'' as he stared a spell for any sign of movement. When there wasn't any, Longarm went back along the ledge for his hat, Topsy, and his derringer. They went down to the canyon floor the safer way, and moved downstream to see what Longarm, or just a guilty conscience, had wrought.

The hat was weathered black felt. The rifle was an eleven-shot .44-40 Bullard Repeater. Longarm had no idea who the face between them belonged to, until Topsy went over to kick the dead man in the ribs and cuss him in Ho. When Longarm asked how come, the Pima gal said the rascal had raped poor Porevo.

Longarm marveled, ''That's Lester Twill in the dead flesh? Well, I'll be switched with snakes if this don't raise more questions than it answers!''

So he lit a cheroot and studied some, despite Topsy's bitching that they'd never done anything but kill people up in those ruins.

He was working on a third cheroot and he'd fit all the pieces more than one way by the time they heard hoofbeats and voices coming up the canyon.

Clio Hendersen rode in with Little Eva, two Pima men,

and four white men, dressed for riding but expensively, in broadloom wool with linen shirtsleeves. When they spotted Longarm and Topsy standing over the cadaver of Lester Twill, they loped in the rest of the way, everybody yelling at once. Clio dropped off her paint pony to run over and drop to her knees by the body, calling out orders to her Indian sidekicks.

But Topsy yelled *"Ka!"* which meant "No!" and launched into her own considerable speech. It had a more calming effect on the other Pima than it did the fat Clio Hendersen, who got to her feet and raised a hand to hit Topsy before she thought better of it, smiled like a shit-eating dog, and asked in English what they were fussing about. She told Longarm she was surprised and upset to see Lester, of all people, lying dead on her mining claim.

Longarm replied firmly but not unkindly, "No, you ain't, Miss Clio. You knew where you'd sent him to lay low, or in this case high, up a cliff where nobody should have looked for him."

A black-bearded white man who'd ridden over from Tombstone with her demanded, "What's going on here! Are you saying this young gent on the ground was laying for us over here, Deputy Long?"

Longarm shook his head and replied, "Not hardly, Mr. Schieffelin. Had not I stumbled over Lester Twill here, he'd have stayed up yonder and just hugged himself for being so clever whilst his wife sold you shares in their salted claim."

The famous Ed Schieffelin gasped. "That's Lester Twill, the villain this little lady accused of trying to jump her claim with a forged wedding certificate?"

Longarm resisted the temptation to dispute the crestfallen Clio's size as he calmly replied, "Weren't all of us more worried about who was telling the truth about that wedding than whether the silver claim they seemed to be fighting over was worth the coin silver dissolved in sulfuric acid a man who worked in an assay office likely used?"

Another potential investor, who turned out to be the real L. J. Wentworth from Virginia City, said, "They were smart enough to use a fistful of pennies as well. The ore samples *I* had assayed ran about thirty-percent copper with a dab of zinc. But are you saying the two of them were lying when each called the other a liar?"

Longarm smiled sheepishly up at the mounted men and confessed, "It worked on me too. I wasted a heap of time trying to prove their wedding never took place. It's tough to detect forgeries or ringers good enough to fool likely part-Indian Mexican neighbors when such foolery never happened. The white JP was willing to concede a big fat gal might be pure Pima and older than her groom—sorry about that, Miss Clio. But her true reason for signing his file copy with an illiterate's attested mark was to make us all suspect exactly what we all suspected. She doubtless insisted he really marry her lest he really try and double-cross her."

Clio moved toward her own pony with surprising grace for her size. But one of the Pima men hung onto its reins and said something firm in Ho to her. So she sank to her fat knees in the gravel and commenced to weep and wail.

Longarm explained, "Pima don't hold with lying, and she must have just said something about me they ain't buying. Miss Topsy here was with me when Lester Twill fired first."

The fat breed gal glared at Longarm through her parted fingers to blubber, "You're the big fibber! Neither my *skookumchuk* nor me meant you any harm, and now you've killed him and said terrible things about the two of us!"

Wentworth dryly remarked, "I understood the two of you were on the outs with one another over this silver claim you were about to show us, Miss Clio. Who was that clown pretending to be me who tried to gun you the other night, Deputy Long?"

Longarm said, "We're still working on that. One of 'em works out as a hired gun from up Utah way. I don't reckon

Lester here feels like telling us where we might find the two who got away.''

Clio Twill née Hendersen sobbed; ''You can't prove that! I asked Lester, and he denied shooting my one real friend from my school days, or having those men trying to murder you! We were only trying to have a little fun over here on my daddy's old claim!''

Longarm explained, ''She means her daddy's old claim that didn't pan out when she asked Lester Twill to survey and assay it for her. Do I have to lecture you silver-mining gents on how often you get a light foam of silver salts bubbling up out of Arizona bedrock? Once the handsome devil found no silver mine after all, he courted and won the owner of the claim along with some real but played-out placers down by Yuma. They knew you generous-hearted gents would never try to take advantage of a breed-orphan who was fighting off a mighty ruthless assay man who'd brought in high-grade samples but wanted to hold back on selling shares before he could literally screw her out of her rich silver mine.''

The bearded Ed Schieffelin decided he'd been playing three-card monte with experts, and asked Clio if she wanted to show them that outcrop her dear old dad had found now.

She told him to go fuck himself.

The biggest frog in the Tombstone puddle made a wry face and declared, ''I'd say you have the goods on her, Deputy Long. But have you enough evidence to convict her of murder as well as this mighty clever confidence game?''

To which Longarm could only reply, ''Nope. But Lester here won't ever harm anyone again, and she's out of business as a social outcast to both her daddy's kind and her mamma's nation.''

He stared down at the weeping fat woman and advised, ''If I were you and didn't want to kill myself, I reckon I'd just saddle up and ride on indefinitely, ma'am. Lord knows you'd have a tough time competing with the other ladies along Sixth Street at the only trade left to you in Tombstone now.''

One of the other investors from town offered her five hundred for her house and lot, take it or leave it. The next time she rose to try for her pony, Topsy said something and none of the Pima tried to stop her. L. J. Wentworth asked who owned this canyon now.

Longarm pointed up at the roofless cliff dwellings above them to say, ''The Hohokam, I reckon. Ain't really anything up here for anybody else. Whole bottom likely floods after a thunderstorm, and no Indians seem to fancy living on the side of cliffs these days.''

He pointed down at the dead body of Lester Twill and added, ''He'll keep until I wire the sheriff in Tucson and see if they want to fight the buzzards for him. We're outside the jurisdiction of Marshal White, and I doubt my office would want the whole can of worms as a gift.''

The disgraced Porevo mounted her pony to ride down the canyon as everyone else, red and white, followed Longarm and Topsy up to where they'd left their own mounts.

Topsy, walking beside him, said, ''Porevo was very naughty. It must have been her Saltu blood. But why did she have her man shoot her own Saltu friend, Lorena? Was she afraid the Saltu girl knew something she had told her was a lie?''

Longarm replied, ''We may never know for certain, now that Lester Twill lies dead back there. She says she never ordered it. I'm sort of inclined to believe her. I don't think Miss Lorena could have had any idea she was being used as a pawn.''

Topsy asked, ''What's a pawn? Did you ever fuck her? Was she any good at that?''

Longarm sighed and said, ''That's something else I'll never know. Lester might have killed her, or had her killed, out of simple green-eyed jealousy. The two gals had been good friends. Clio might have kept talking about this until a man who wanted her and everything she owned all to himself might have snapped. It's tougher to solve such a killing when the killer hasn't got a really bright reason. There was this trash family up Kansas way who killed travelers passing by just for their small change, pocket watches, or fresh socks. So it took the law forever to notice they were even killing folks. Their name was Bender. The case has never been officially closed.''

It would have been bragging to speculate on whether some vicious trash he'd once accounted for in the Nebraska Sand Hills might have been long-sought and crazy-mean Benders.

As they got to the saddle mules, Ed Schieffelin suggested they all dismount and let their own mounts water and rest up before they rode back to Tombstone in the cool of the evening.

When Longarm allowed that made a heap of sense, Topsy took Little Eva aside, and the two of them approached Longarm to see if he wanted to explore those cliff dwellings with the two of them.

He pointed out that while their male Pima pals might not follow them up yonder, nosy Saltu had been known to poke about in old ruins for arrowheads and pottery. The two of them looked so crestfallen, he told them he had his choice of two hotel rooms back in town, and once he'd snuck them up the back stairs of the Cosmopolitan, it was just as well that strawberry blond had suddenly become way too famous for him.

Chapter 21

He'd promised John Clum the inside story. So Longarm met with him the next morning in the Capitol Saloon, up from Clum's *Epitaph*, for a sit-down at a corner table with a pitcher of beer.

Clum said the convoluted plot to interest investors in a salted silver strike seemed just too ... convoluted. He asked Longarm, "Why did they murder Lorena Webber after they'd recruited her as a tool to spread the word they were fighting over a valuable claim? It seems to me they'd have been better off with her still alive and still telling anyone who'd listen that Lester Twill was out to diddle her old school chum out of a lode to rival the Lucky Cuss or Tough Nut!"

Longarm fished out a couple of smokes to enjoy with their beer as he replied, "What seems to make sense to us seems dumb to crooks. If crooks thought like you and me, they wouldn't be crooks, John. Neither one of us would have murdered anybody or hired at least half a dozen gun-slicks if all we'd had in mind was a con game."

Clum was good. He cocked a brow and demanded, "Half a dozen? I made it five. The three you shot and the two who got away down past the Mountain Maid works."

Longarm modestly replied, "I only shot two. One caught

it from a pal. Crooks are like that. You forgot the one who blew himself up trying to blow me up in Saguaro Wells before I could get down here.''

John Clum accepted a cheroot with a silent nod of thanks, and then asked, ''Why? Wasn't it awfully dumb for them to involve a federal lawman miles away in their get-rich-quick scheme? Had they left you the the hell alone, you'd have never heard about Clio Hendersen's silver strike over in Chindi Canyon, right?''

Longarm thumbnailed a match head aflame for both their cheroots as he replied, ''Not exactly. I'd already talked to the late Lorena Webber and they didn't know what she might have told me.''

He leaned forward to light Clum's smoke as he added, ''It's too late to ask Lester Twill, and Clio Hendersen now denies she really knew the father who left her that marginal silver claim. But Lester might have worried about just how smart an old school chum might really be, and it could have unsettled him when Lorena wired from Tucson that she was riding farther afield to seek outside help.''

Clum took a drag on his cheroot while he thought that over. Then he nodded and said, ''I see what you mean about the futility of trying to fathom a dead mind. Suffice it to say, the clever rascal who'd have known how to add color to a low-grade strike and mastermind such a devious confidence game won't be doing anything like that again. His pathetic Pima partner in crime has been put out of business, whether she knew anything about those hired guns or not.''

Clum sipped some beer and pointed out, ''Two of *those* rascals are still at large, and they owe you for what you did to their pals.''

Longarm shrugged and replied, ''A lot of rascals must think *I* owe *them*. That goes with packing any badge. No lawman would *pack* a badge if he worried about all the rascals who've said they were going to get you when they got out.''

"Doesn't that happen?" asked the newspaper man.

Longarm shrugged and said, "Surprisingly seldom, considering. The first time I pulled prison chasing in the army, the ragged-ass guardhouse lawyers I had chopping stove wood for the mess hall assured me they'd be waiting for me in the dark some night, once they were out of the guardhouse. But the next time I saw them in town, they wanted to buy me a drink. Those last two guns Lester recruited are likely out of the territory and worried more about their next meal right now. I don't know what Lester promised 'em. But they're not going to get it now, even if they come back for a rematch and win."

Clum smiled at the picture and mused aloud, "That might endanger a growing reputation's health. I see what you meant about those guardhouse lawyers. There'd be little profit and lots of risk if outlaws started going after lawmen instead of less dangerous and more prosperous victims. But doesn't it irk you that for all you know one of the killers who got away could have been the one who murdered Miss Lorena Webber?"

Longarm grimaced and said, "It irks me that Frank, Jesse, the Kid, and a whole shithouse full of murderous sons of bitches are at large as well. But what would I do for a living if all the crooks in this land of opportunity were in jail? I've tried herding cows and mining coal and hardrock. The job I have with the Justice Department is more fun."

Clum laughed, and asked what Longarm meant to do next, seeing he'd wound things up in Tombstone.

Longarm sighed and said, "I got one last dolorous chore down this way. Seeing my prisoner up in Saguaro Wells is still healing up, I have the time as well as the duty to attend Miss Lorena's funeral in the morning. Tomorrow being the sabbath and her kith and kin coming in from all around to see her off."

Clum hesitated, then said, "The florist across from the undertaker offered me a news tip I'm not going to run. He says you sprang for a handsome horseshoe of yellow roses.''

Longarm shrugged and replied, ''Well, she was from Texas and liked to ride. So what else should I have sent over to the undertaker's?''

John Clum looked away and said he and his wife would be there the next day.

So they finished their beer and each went his way. Longarm headed for the Western Union to bring Marshal Vail up to date on his travel plans. Then he legged it for the nearby office of the stage line to see about a ride up to Saguaro Wells for himself and his old McClellan saddle. For while riding astride was more comfortable by far, it took longer to get there once you started talking about more than, say, ten miles. For whether it was packing a rider or hauling a coach, a horse or mule was good for no more than ten miles or so before it had to stop and rest up a good while.

That was how come stagecoaches had been invented. It wasn't the *coach* that moved faster than a saddle mount. It was the stages, or ten-to-fifteen-mile runs between stations, where spent teams could be exchanged for fresh ones, that allowed the coach to roll on and on at an average of nine miles an hour, getting you there much sooner than anything but a railroad train.

It hadn't gotten all that hot as yet that morning, and he'd left his frock coat at the Cosmopolitan, once he'd shooed Little Eva and Topsy down the back steps and over to the Dexter Livery's hayloft for now. But the sun was high enough by then to lean sort of heavy on a man's shoulders, so he cut across to the shady side.

As he was doing so he absently admired his own reflection in the plate glass of Syndow & Kicke's Clothing Store. Being modest-natured, he wasn't staring too tight at his own image when the portly figure on the sunlit walk behind him slapped leather.

They both fired at the same time. The man who'd introduced himself as L. J. Wentworth in that half-built warehouse fired at where Longarm had just been. Longarm fired from one knee a good three yards down the street and nailed his more stationary target just over the heart.

The beefy hired gun bounced off the brick wall behind him to fall forward like a tree cut off at the roots. But Longarm wasn't looking at him when he landed in the street to raise a cloud of dust and dry horseshit.

Longarm had thrown his upper body the other way as he fired at a *second* target, who was aiming at him from the open doorway to the first one's left. That one jackknifed around the .44 slug Longarm put into his guts, and wound up in a moaning heap on the walk. So Longarm rose and followed his smoking gun muzzle back across the street to see what they'd wanted.

As he joined the one still breathing in the doorway of a saddle shop, a crowd began to gather at a respectful distance. One of old Fred White's deputies edged closer to ask what was going on.

Longarm said he was trying to find out. He kicked the fallen man's Colt Lightning .41 inside the shop and asked, "What's going on, old son? How come the two of you stayed so long at the fair?"

The man lying in a fetal position on his left side in chinked chaps and an old blue army shirt moaned, "We had to pay you back for gunning our boss, you hop-around gob of spit-on-a-stove!"

Longarm replied, "Your loyalty is touching as well as unusual, you poor dumb shit. How did you figure he was going to pay you after he was dead? And for the record, I never gunned him. He fell of a cliff."

The one he'd gunned for certain didn't answer. Longarm hunkered down to feel the side of his throat and make sure he couldn't. Then he got back to his feet and began to reload as he told the town deputy that seemed to be the final chapter to a needlessly wild story. Marshal White himself came along a few minutes later to tell Longarm not to board that stage before he'd given a full depositon for the deputy coroner. He added he was sorry it was a Saturday.

Longarm said, "I meant to leave Monday in any case. Got to attend that funeral tomorrow, and who'd want to roll into Saguaro Wells on a Sunday evening?"

So they shook on it, and the local law got to work on cleaning up the mess so the street could get back to business before everyone closed for the day at noon.

Longarm drifted over to the Dexter Livery to invite those frisky Pima gals to spend the coming siesta with him, seeing his hotel room would have been cleaned up by the Mexican maids by now. But when he got to the Dexter, they told him neither Little Eva nor Topsy had shown that morning as Longarm had suggested.

He reflected as he went to scout up his noon dinner that neither gal was under direct orders from him. But this was a hell of a time to find out he'd be spending La Siesta alone, all tensed up after a gunfight and feeling wistful about the coming funeral and what might have been.

Inhaling frijoles and a beef enchilada at the Can-Can near his hotel, Longarm reflected on the little time he'd spent with the late Lorena Webber, and told himself not to indulge in wet daydreams about her or her more shapely older sister, the Widow Cleveland. The one was dead and the other likely spoken for if he'd read the gleam in her foreman's eye correctly. Young Bobby MacBean had the inside track as a neighbor boy from Texas who'd known both sisters, in the Bible sense or not. They'd both be at the funeral come morning. Trying to compete with old Bobby would make him look stupid, even if he won.

He ambled back to the Cosmopolitan for lack of any place better to go as the sun rose ever higher. When he got up to his hired room, he saw it was just as well he hadn't hauled two half-clad Pima gals along. Two Mexican maids were still messing around in there. The bed was remade and one gal was just standing there as the other dusted. They both looked shyly down at the floor as the dusting

174

one murmured they were all through and sorry if they'd upset him.

Longarm ticked his hat brim and allowed they hadn't upset him at all. Had he said that in Border Mexican the one just standing there might not have murmured, *"Imagino que es un amante tremendo y que sabe chicar como loco."*

To which Longarm felt obliged to reply with a gallant bow, *"Muchas gracias, querida."*

So they both ran out of the room, squealing like pigs, albeit the younger one hadn't been so bad.

Longarm shut the door in restored good humor. It wasn't every day a pretty gal said she thought a man was likely a tremendous lover who'd fuck like mad.

He hung up his six-gun and peeled off his vest and shirt to wash up in the corner. He'd just shuttered the windows against the glare outside when he heard timorous tapping on the door.

It wasn't the younger and skinnier of the two Mexican maids. It was the plumper one with the dirtier mouth. She'd been crying. When he asked how come, she sobbed, "Helena says she thinks you may be El Brazo Largo. I did not even know you spoke Spanish!"

Longarm gently said, "I suspected as much, Señorita. There's no reason for either of us to cry about what you said. You were just funning and I took it as a compliment."

"You are not angry that I intimated you were a wild man in bed?" she asked, with smoke signals rising in her sort of Indian eyes.

He circled her, shirtless, and quietly shut the door to the hall as he asked, "Why should I be sore? The truth never hurt anybody with nothing to feel ashamed of."

So she was all over him, and by the time they were across the bed with the skirts of her simple maid's uniform up around her waist with nothing under it and his pants down around his boots, he'd learned they called her Gordita downstairs, and even though they didn't need a pillow un-

175

der her ass, he sincerely felt Gordita or Little Fatty was a needlessly mean nickname for a gal whose smooth taffy-colored skin was just well filled with what felt like marsh-mallow, where it was dry. The slit between her pleasantly plump thighs felt more like a hot tamale when he entered it with his old organ-grinder.

It felt even better, all over, once they'd died together, as the Mexicans put it, and shucked every stitch to start all over in the dimly lit room.

She said it was her siesta time too. So he asked her if she had plans for later that night when she got off work. Gordita sighed and said she had somebody coming to escort her home directly.

A familiar gray cat got up in Longarm's gut to turn around twice and switch its bushy tail as he asked in des-perately casual Spanish whether she was married up or spo-ken for.

She sighed again and said neither one exactly. She'd told the fool who'd be meeting her at midnight that she didn't fancy him. But some hombres just wouldn't take no for an answer, and she was afraid he might get hurt or hurt some-body if he thought she fancied someone else more than him.

Longarm held Gordita closer as he mused aloud that some hombres could sure be stubborn, once they'd set their mind on a *muchacha*.

Then he sat up straighter and said, "Son of a bitch! There it was, staring me in the face like a boil on a pretty gal's nose, and I was too blind to *see* it!"

Gordita timidly asked if she'd said something wrong.

He kissed her, then kissed a tit and ran his hand down to pet her ring-dang-doo as he replied, "Not hardly! You said something right! You may have pointed out one piece of the picture that solves the whole damned puzzle!"

Chapter 22

Most mornings found Longarm feeling overdressed in the three-piece tobacco-tweed suit the dress regulations of President Hayes had forced on federal officials. But that Saturday morning he went back to Syndow & Kicke's to see if they'd hire him something more formal for Miss Lorena's funeral. They told him they didn't hire out clothes as a rule, but they loaned him a vest and a clawhammer coat, with striped trousers, as a courtesy to one of their outstanding cattlewomen. He insisted on paying for a new linen shirt to wear under the fancy vest. It was the least he could do to make up for that bullet hole through their big front window.

When he got to First Methodist on fancy foot, he found a good-sized crowd milling about. Most of them were cattle folk, and not all of them were Methodists. He'd heard Johnny Ringo was of the Hebrew persuasion, and he knew Curly Bill was a Papist. He didn't ask what the Clantons might be. The crusty old cuss in the Texas hat along with Ike Clanton and his two younger brothers, had all put on fresh shirts and clean bandannas for the occasion. Ike Clanton hailed Longarm over, and once he'd shook all around, Longarm told them what he'd figured out so far. Old Man Clanton looked as if he was fixing to cry as he described the various ways he'd like to fix the cowardly son of a bitch who'd shoot a young lady of quality with a buffalo rifle.

Then the crowd commenced to move inside while Longarm was still talking with the Clantons. He managed to work his way to another aisle and sit closer to the front behind Lorena's sister, Miss Melony, Bobby MacBean, and some other riders off the Running W.

The closed coffin was in front of the altar behind the floral tributes from all over. Longarm felt sort of proud of his big horseshoe of yellow roses until he spotted a clay *olla* with a single red cactus flower and a penciled card you had to strain to read. Once he did, standing up behind Melony and MacBean as if to adjust his underwear, he saw the message read, *"Afligido, me patrona,"* or, "I'm sorry, boss lady." So Longarm sat back down with a lump in his throat as he tried not to picture exactly what lay inside that lead-lined coffin. Like Old Man Clanton had said, she'd been quality.

Like all funerals, this one was too short for some, and droned on too long for others. Folks Longarm didn't know got up to say nice things about a nice gal and wish her nice sister well in carrying on at the Running W. Then they got to sing some hymns, and Miss Melony turned around to see who was singing "Farther Along" in such a loud but not unpleasant baritone. When she saw it was Longarm, she smiled and turned back to her own hymnal. But when they'd all finished, she must have said something to the man at her side, because Bobby MacBean turned to look him over and then nod pleasantly enough.

Longarm had deliberately sat where nobody could bend his ear, and he didn't approach anybody once the ceremony inside the church was over and they all had to sit in silence while the pallbearers took Miss Lorena out to the church-yard ahead of them.

Longarm let the others file out after the coffin, starting

from the first row of mourners as if the crowd was turning inside out.

When he finally got over to the grave site, they'd already lowered the coffin on ropes, and Miss Melony was gently scattering a silver dipper full of dry dusty dirt from the pile beside the grave down into it. She handed the dipper to Bobby MacBean, who followed suit and handed it on to an older Mexican in a silver-mounted *charro* outfit and a brace of Colt '73's. Longarm didn't press forward to take part in that rite. He knew the sextons would finish burying her with *their* shovels, and he had other fish to fry. So he just stood with his hat in his hands until everyone had had their say and made their gestures. Then he turned and headed back out to the dusty unpaved street at a respectful pace as others passed him or lagged behind. He made it out to the sun-baked street in front of the bare gravel churchyard before Bobby MacBean caught up with him to remark, "Young Billy Clanton just told me you'd said you doubted either of those men you shot it out with yesterday morning had anything to do with Miss Lorena's murder. Does that mean you suspect somebody else?"

Longarm stopped and turned to face MacBean as he calmly replied, "I know who it was. I just don't know how to prove it, Bob."

The lean but muscular ramrod smiled uncertainly and demanded, "Who do you think it was? Rules of evidence don't apply when somebody kills a neighbor from Texas!"

Longarm shook his head and said, "If I wanted to try the case in front of Judge Lynch, I'd have told the Clantons. But like I told them when they made the same offer, I mean to settle the case my own way, Bob."

MacBean glanced down thoughtfully and asked, "How? I notice you don't seem to be wearing that .44-40 you usually pack whilst after outlaws, Deputy Long."

Longarm said, "My friends call me Custis. I left my side arm back at the Cosmopolitan Hotel with my other coat. It rode awkward under this one, and I notice you and half your riders here are wearing your own guns, so I reckon at least some of you would protect me if push came to shove. I came here to pay my respect to Miss Lorena, not to arrest nobody."

MacBean nodded thoughtfully and decided, "That means the last man in that gang couldn't be anywhere around here, right?"

Longarm said, "Wrong. The one who shot Miss Lorena had nothing to do with any of the others I've brushed with down this way so far. Unless I'm mistaken, he was working on his own, and Lorena Webber's death had nothing to do with that confidence game her old school chum was using her to pull off. Lorena Webber was murdered most foul by a dirty little coward she trusted as much as she trusted Clio Hendersen."

"Is he anywhere near here?" MacBean repeated insistently.

Longarm nodded and said, "He is. But this is neither the time nor place to arrest anybody. I have the shithead's number, and I can pick him up any time I have a little more proof to present in court."

He added, "In the meantime, I want to get this claw-hammer coat back to its rightful owners before I sweat it up. So we'd best talk some more about crime and punishment later, Bob."

He turned away, his mouth as dry and tasty as the bottom of an empty flower pot, while his heart raced inside him like a wound-up skitter-mouse. Then sure enough, he heard the dulcet roar of six-guns, more than one, and whirled with his double derringer out to see Bobby MacBean face-down in the dust with the back of his own frock coat on fire as Old Man Clanton and two of his three sons pumped round after round into the already thoroughly dead son of a bitch.

Longarm couldn't get a word in edgewise until they'd all run out of ammunition and MacBean's blood was running along the berm of the street in a sluggish stream. Once he could make himself heard above the ringing in his ears,

Longarm called out, "I asked you to try and take him *alive,* dad blast it!"

Ike Clanton came forward, holding out Longarm's gun-belt, as he replied with a grin, "You sure have hair on your chest, Longarm. You *said* he'd try to backshoot you if he was the guilty one, and you *still* gave him the chance!"

Longarm took his six-gun back with a nod of thanks as he replied, "I had to. He might have been innocent and I needed more proof if he was guilty. That's why I asked you friends of Miss Lorena to watch my back whilst I spooked her killer."

By now others had gathered the grit to circle in closer. Melony Cleveland née Webber ran forward to stare wildly down at her shot-up foreman, turn her blazing eyes on Old Man Clanton, and scream, "What have you done, you murderous old lunatic? I didn't believe what I read about you and your outlaw brood in the *Epitaph,* but now I see it's all *true!* You're all mad dogs and I'll get you, get you, *get* you all for this!"

Old Man Clanton scuffed a boot in the dust and murmured, "Gee whiz, it wasn't my fault, ma'am."

So Longarm chimed in. "Hold your fire, Miss Melony. What Mr. Clanton and his boys just done was at my request."

She whirled to demand, "*You* told these murderous stock thieves to murder poor Bobby MacBean?"

Longarm strapped his own side arm back in place as he quietly told her, "No, ma'am. I asked them to watch my back, and that's all they were doing when your foreman made his confession to the murder of your kid sister by going for his own guns."

Melony stared down in horror at the horrid hash they'd made of MacBean as she gasped, "Bobby MacBean, the boy next door and foreman of her Running W, was the one who shot poor Lorena? Why, why? In the name of God, *why?*"

Longarm saw others had crowded closer to hear, so he

raised his voice an octave as he calmly explained, "He done it in the name of love, Miss Melony. I don't mean he killed your kid sister because he loved *her*. He was in love with *you*, back in Texas, all the time he was helping her build up her fine herd out this way. But you were married up to another. Or, that is, you *were* until your sister told him about you being widowed and alone back in Texas. She doubtless told him you were too proud to take charity, and wouldn't come out here to live as a poor relation where he could start courting her some more. So when your sister took up another cause for Miss Clio Hendersen and took to riding all over the desert with Indians, he saw the chance to bring down a flock of birds with one rifle ball. He and likely he alone knew where your sister would be all the time because she was keeping in touch with her own outfit by wire. After he rode out alone to ambush her, he tore into Tombstone to wire you in Texas that your sister was dead, knowing you'd come right out to take over and he'd have the inside track with a gal he loved for her ownself, but was rich on top of her other charms."

Old Man Clanton asked, "What put you on to him, *amigo mio*?"

Longarm said, "Elimination, to begin with. Killing Miss Lorena made no sense if the motive was a confidence game or the killing of yours truly. After that, I kept getting back to how sudden Miss Melony got out here. It only worked if Bob there wired her about her sister before those Pima ever carried Miss Lorena in to Tombstone. But as you heard me tell him just now. I needed more proof, and thanks to you and yours, he gave it to us on a silver platter."

But back in Denver, once Longarm arrived with the recovered but soon-to-be-late Blacky Barnes, the crusty old Marshal Billy Vail wanted more than that to explain what in thunder had been going on.

Seated behind his cluttered desk in his oak-paneled inner office while Longarm searched in vain for an ashtray near the leather chair he was seated in himself, Vail growled,

"*Bueno*. A fat Pima breed of means asks a so-far-unlucky mining man to assay this mining claim left to her by her never-quite-made-it daddy. Lester Twill knows enough about prospecting to see the traces of silver ore up in Chindi Canyon ain't worth developing. But working in an assay office, he'd know how to dissolve silver, copper, and maybe zinc fishing sinkers in sulfuric acid, pack the acid over to the low-grade strike, and pour it slow to seep into the low-grade ore and enrich the shit out of it as the alkili in the rock turns the acid to silver-copper-zinc sulfide.

"I can see how they'd hesitate to go for an out-and-out sale or even a grubstake deal without something to lull the natural suspicions of mining men rich enough to matter. So, seeing you can't cheat an honest man, but big money boys are ever ready to move in like sharks when they smell blood in the water, the two of 'em staged that crazy domestic scene, knowing it would occasion a whole lot of gossip and establish the suspicion that whatever Lester Twill was after, it was more likely her silver mine than her fat ass!"

Longarm flicked some tobacco ash on the floor, hoping it was good for rug mites, as he replied, "That's about the size of it, Boss. I told the local lawmen what they'd been up to. I didn't see how Judge Dickerson down the hall had any jurisdiction in that case."

Vail growled, "I see you let the coroner in Tucson tidy up after the Clanton Gang, seeing both the late Robert MacBean and his victim, Lorena Webber, were residents of Pima County. So who in blue thunder were all those hired guns working for if they weren't working for Lester Twill, Clio Hendersen, or that shit who murdered his own boss lady so's he could court her big sister?"

Longarm took a drag on his cheroot and innocently asked, "Didn't Henry, out front, type that in? I thought it was obvious, once the one dying on the walk in Tombstone told me they'd been out to get me for gunning their boss."

Vail snapped, "Don't play games with me, asshole."

183

Longarm smiled sheepishly and replied, "To tell the truth, I wanted to let sleeping dogs lie. You're right that I can't tie those outlaws in with anyone around Tombstone. But they're all dead, Lester Twill and Bobby MacBean are dead, and Blacky Barnes will hang for his other crimes, even though I couldn't get him to admit shit on the long train ride from Arizona Territory."

Vail started to ask a dumb question, nodded slowly instead, and said, "You never shot Lester Twill, and even if you had, they came after you way earlier. They had no way of knowing in advance that MacBean was fixing to get hisself shot. So that leaves the outlaw you'd shot so painfully back up in Saguaro Wells!"

Longarm nodded and said, "Blacky Barnes seems to have been more of an outlaw than we gave him credit for. Mormon Jim hailed from up around the Four Corners too. But I doubt they were after me for revenge. They were hoping to take their boss away from anyone you sent to transport him, and I seemed to make them uneasy for some reason."

Billy Vail laughed and said, "They had good reason. You were more dangerous than they feared, and I follow your drift about just letting their boss hang and saving the taxpayers a whole lot of money."

Then he glanced down at the typed onionskins, moving his lips as he tallied some numbers, and said, "There's only one thing I'm still puzzled about. I told you to come on home while Barnes healed up in Saguaro Wells. Yet you stayed down in Tombstone all that time after you'd solved the murder of Lorena Webber?"

Longarm flicked more ash on the rug as he calmly replied, "Wasn't in Tombstone *all* that time. Had to ride out to the Running W to sort of console her big sister some."

Vail cocked a brow and demanded, "You needed that much time just to console the dead gal's sister? How much consoling might one such sister need, for Pete's sake?''

To which Longarm could only reply, ''A heap, Boss. She seemed sort of emotional, once I got to consoling her out yonder.''

Watch for

LONGARM AND THE WRONGED WOMAN

248th novel in the exciting LONGARM series
from Jove

Coming in August!